PARTISANS

PETER MATTHIESSEN

PARTISANS

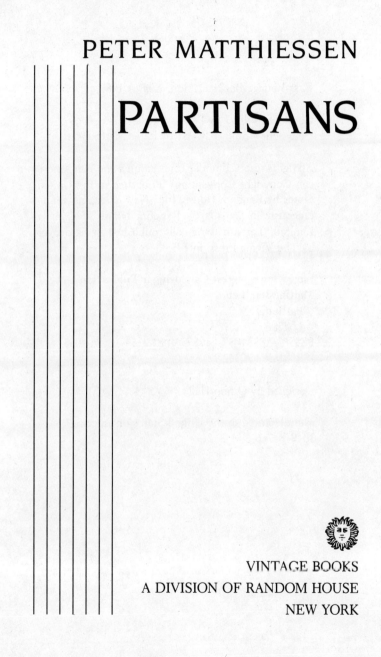

VINTAGE BOOKS

A DIVISION OF RANDOM HOUSE

NEW YORK

Library of Congress Cataloging-in-Publication Data
Matthiessen, Peter.
    Partisans.
    I. Title.
PS3563.A8584P37   1987   813'.54   86-40557
ISBN 0-394-75342-9

Designed by Quinn Hall

Manufactured in the United States of America
10 9 8 7 6 5 4 3 2 1

You see, to love the universal man necessarily means to despise and, at times, to hate the real man standing at your side.

—FEODOR DOSTOEVSKI, *Diaries*

For every mistake of our adversaries, a part, more or less large, of the responsibility is ours. We are responsible for the good we haven't done, for the bad we have not prevented.

—A. ROSSI, *Physiologie du P.C.F.*

PARTISANS

1

Sand was asleep for the seventh time when, early one morning that September, the first report came in. On the night desk of the wire service the old French telephone stood black and scrawny, and vibrant with irritation, like a rooster. He seized it, and a sharp street voice scratched out at him, driving him back from the receiver.

His response was remote, way off somewhere beyond his sleepiness. In answering he had lifted his hand from page eight of his book, and watched pages seven, six, five, four, three, two, and one flip forward and lie flat, until only the flyleaf was exposed. He knew he had got nowhere, and would have to start all over again from the beginning.

"Please say that again," his voice complained. "One language at a time."

The informant was very excited. He repeated several times that his name was Alex and that Sand's superior should be notified at once, but he refused to bare the source of his information. Sand had been in postwar Paris long enough not to insist on the latter point.

"You say Jacobi has been purged." He rubbed his fingers against his forehead, then reached across the book for his cigarettes. On the flyleaf his name, inscribed with an attention that had not been paid the book, seemed as unreal to Sand as the sound of his own voice. It belonged to a man in mirrors whose face seemed more foolish every day.

Barney Sand—Paris, 1953.

Barney Sand, he thought—who in hell is that?

"Yes," said the voice, "I know who Jacobi is, monsieur, but I don't know who *you* are. I just can't take your word alone for a story as important as this. . . . No, I'm not making fun of you, believe me."

Barney Sand was a merry old soul, and a merry old soul was he—ping! He lashed at the scraggy apparatus with his pencil.

"A-l-e-x. Alex. Thanks very much, Alex. I'll have him call you back." Sand studied the sated telephone, then seized it again, as if to take it by surprise, and telephoned his editor. "Sorry to wake you," he said. "You're to call Alex. A-l-e-x."

"I can spell it," the editor said. "What's the goddam hurry?"

"Jacobi. He's been expelled. They're keeping him in hiding, and they're keeping it quiet. No police, no press."

"You have the number?"

"What number?"

"Alex. A-l-e-x, remember?"

"He says you have it. You're to call in half an hour, at his place. He says it was dangerous for him where he was."

"Look, I'll be over in twenty minutes. You meet me in the café there on the corner, and order me black coffee. And get that number out of my notebook, top right-hand drawer of my desk. Under 'C,' for contacts. Look up 'Alex.'"

"How do you spell that?"

"Backward," the editor said. "Look, Barney, it's four o'clock in the morning. At four o'clock in the morning nothing in the world can make me laugh. Now get moving, this is important."

Sand replaced the receiver, smiling, then stopped smiling and stood up. In an outer office of the wire service the telegraph, untended, tickered on, placing words on yellow tape and the tape in wire baskets. This was the dead hour, and he tasted the stale air of it in his mouth. He closed the unread book, drew his crumpled jacket from the back of his chair, and wandered slowly to the inner offices, where he found the contact's number. Then, heels clicking on the concrete steps, he went downstairs.

On the street he stepped on his cigarette, stared at it for a moment, then shook himself wide awake. The fresh air of morning cleared his head, and he felt a recurrent elation at departing from the office, as if this time, at long last, he had forsaken a drab routine forever.

But elation came and went with the same breath.

Jacobi, he thought, how very sad that is. But he pictured an abstract, international Jacobi, a Jacobi of newspapers and ticker tapes, and not the man he once had known, whose defeat, if such it was, could not be thought about so much as felt, like a sign of winter.

Sand started at a feline brush of fur across one shoulder and, turning, found himself confronted by a woman. He had no idea where she had come from, she was simply there, a lavender apparition, and standing much too close. But she did not trouble to solicit him. She only stared him in the eye, her powdered face pinched back in a tattered hank of fur to hide the bad teeth of a bad old age, which even drunks despised, and which would keep her in the street all night and for many nights to come. No, she meant simply to challenge his aloneness with her own, and waited.

Startled, he peered into her eyes again, but this time they shone red and runny and gave back nothing. The spell was banished by a waft of garlic from the lacquered mouth.

"Mademoiselle, it's very late," he said to her in French,

and pressed one hundred francs to her cold hand. But she only watched him, drifting back against the building as he drew away from her.

Sand moved rapidly toward the café on the corner. In the pale pink dawn of Paris, chill with new autumn air, he listened to his footsteps ringing out behind him, like some persistent second self of solitude.

2

Sand had known Jacobi in the one way Jacobi could be known, in violent passing.

The year was 1938. Edwin Baring Sand, then a boy of fourteen, was with his parents in the south of France, where they had come by car from Spain. Sand's father, an American consul, had decided in April to leave the country. A few weeks before, the armies had parted Spain along the Ebro River, and crossing high above the lines in a special plane, the boy peered down at war, and, innocent, saw only the slow smoke of it, silent, without smell. He wondered if soldiers in the sun below had squinted up at the silver shape slipping swiftly away toward the north.

At Barcelona a borrowed car awaited them. It was a big black Mercedes, sulky with neglect, and it took them on into Catalonia, complaining. The distance to the frontier was less than a hundred miles, and they got off to an early start; yet because of the refugees in the roads and because the Mercedes ran according to a schedule of its own, midday found them just beyond Gerona. Near the ancient fortifications of that town the Mercedes stalled and would go no farther. A monument in the middle of the road, it dammed a band of refugees, which built up behind, then overflowed around it—

rude carts and barrows, bicycles and baby carriages, all creeping north, away from war, toward France.

But for the burros and the litter of belongings, the caravan
might have been a funeral procession. The men wore berets
and black Sunday suits, and the women were uniform in black
crepe dresses, black shawls and stockings, and black shoes
scuffed with dust. The children, in gray-brown for the most
part, brought up the rear. All moved in stolid silence until they
reached the Mercedes, where the leaders halted, and, to break
the monotony of their journey, pretended they could not get
past. They shouted at one another and at the Mercedes, and
one of them proposed that they all sit down and talk the matter over. But the women, sterner, prodded them from behind,
whereupon the men who had shouted most loudly about the
delay blocked off the rest by pausing parallel with the Mercedes to offer encouragement and advice.

The advice went to Consul Sand, who, sweating and barking his knuckles on the engine, was searching for a loose connection and hoping he would recognize it when he found it.
The encouragement was for the car itself, which was poked
with donkey sticks and had its tires kicked, and for Mrs. Sand,
who, parboiled behind the rolled-up windows, shrank back in
terror of all this coarse good will. She could not imagine why
these refugees she had felt so sorry for back along the road
should now be laughing and tapping on her window. Though
two years in Spain, she remained unacquainted with the Spanish temperament and was convinced that these ruffians, re-
senting the big black limousine, were on the point of
overturning it. There's the Catholic Church for you! she kept
repeating to herself, not quite certain what she meant.

Meanwhile her son Edwin was seated on the roof of the
car, absorbing matters with eyes and ears and nose, like a
squirrel. He was offered a crust of bread, which he declined,
and red wine from a goatskin *bota*, which he accepted. This

Spanish *tinto* was thick and very strong and hot from the sun
of noon, and, as he did not know how to operate the *bota*, he
squirted a large amount of it down his neck and onto his shirt.
The onlookers were delighted. They drank from it flamboy-
antly for his benefit, then passed it along and shoved it under
the nose of Consul Sand, who was clapped smartly on the
back.

Beside himself, the consul straightened up and shouted at
his son. "For God's sake, Edwin, do you have to help these
idiots block the traffic! Must you play the idiot yourself?"

His tone was offensive to the refugees, who moved on after
their women. One man stayed. He had been standing next to
Consul Sand for quite some time, observing the uneven contest with the engine. The consul tinkered a little more with
his letter-knife, then straightened up again, exasperated.

"Is there something about me which interests you?" he
said in Spanish.

"Try your points," the man answered in English. He stood
there, hands in pockets, in the sun, an overcoat slung over his
shoulder, a knapsack beside him on the ground. He was a man
of middle height, and hard in a heavy way, and he wore a
beret and a cheap black suit and a khaki shirt open at the
neck.

"Points?" said Consul Sand.

The man folded the overcoat and placed it, with the knapsack, on the running board. He took the knife from Consul
Sand and ran the blade of it from one sparkplug to the engine
block. With the other hand he reached deep into the machine
and pulled on the lever of the starter. There was no spark. He
then removed the distributor cap and inspected the points.

"Carbon," he said. "You have a nail file?"

Edwin Sand jumped down and asked his mother, who produced one. "Now don't get it all greasy," she called out gaily,
though in fact she felt quite put upon, and all the more so

when the strange man came back and got into the driver's seat without so much as an if-you-please. He carried the nail file like a pirate knife between his teeth.

But the Mercedes, coughing weakly, revived beneath his foot.

"Oh, aren't you wonderful!" cried Mrs. Sand, bent forward. "Now how much do we owe you?"

The man said nothing, nor did he remove himself from the front seat. He handed back the nail file without looking at her, then turned toward the open door and Consul Sand.

"So that's what the trouble was," the consul said. "The points."

"There's other trouble, from the way she sounds."

"Well, the thing should get us to the border." Consul Sand placed one foot on the running board, frowning slightly when the man stayed where he was.

"It may," the man said.

They watched each other, and the boy, watching both of them, drew nearer. His father was red in the face and glaring at the other. The stranger, in turn, did not seem to find this ungrateful. His face was calm and cold, and his black eyes gleamed, unblinking. It was as if some silent contest was being waged, and even Mrs. Sand seemed to sense this, for she said tightly, "Come along, Edwin, get in the back with me."

"You've been very helpful," the consul said at last. "Is there something we can give you?"

Some stragglers from the caravan who were coming up sniffed out the tension between the two. "*Americanos,*" one remarked and shrugged his shoulders. They clustered behind Edwin until, goaded from the rear, they edged along. A burro's head pushed rudely at Edwin, and, shifting his position in order to pat it, he saw why the stranger had already won the contest.

The stranger was shaking his head. "I'll just drive you to

the frontier," he said, "in case the car breaks down again." He was sitting half turned in the open door, exposing beneath the cheap black jacket the butt of a gun in a shoulder holster. When his eyes met Edwin's stare he buttoned the jacket, and, taking the knapsack and overcoat from the running board, slung them in across his lap and down on the floor beside him.

"Yes," said Consul Sand quite loudly, for the benefit of his wife. "Yes, that might be an excellent idea." He went forward and slammed the hood down hard. Returning, he hesitated and, when the stranger did not stir, got into the back seat. Edwin ran around the car and jumped in beside the driver in the front.

The car slipped forward down the long white road.

"You American?" Edwin yawned. The yawn pretended indifference to people's pistols, but went unnoticed by the driver, who nodded, staring straight ahead.

"I am too," the boy said. "My name's Edwin Sand, but I'm called Barney."

One hand lifted slightly from the wheel. It was a large hand, smeared with engine grease.

"Well, what's yours?" the boy asked.

"Smith," the man said, glancing at the rear-view mirror. Barney, turning, saw his father raise his eyebrows. The consul sat with his hands, white-knuckled, on his knees.

When his son introduced his parents to Mr. Smith, the consul said, "Edwin, your mother and I are quite capable of introducing ourselves without your assistance."

"But you didn't know his name, even."

"I still don't," the consul said.

"But listen, I just told you—"

"Sit around and be quiet, Edwin!"

"My parents still call me Edwin," Barney told the driver. They were nearing the peasant caravans again, and the man with the *bota* danced out into the road. When the Mercedes slowed, he sprang onto the running board and shoved the wineskin in at Barney. "Ay, *borracho! Mira!*" he cried. Consul Sand shouted at him, and the Spaniard withdrew his arm, then took the driver's hand. "*Suerte, amigo, suerte a la fronterra!*" He toppled backward against his burro, waving. His companions cheered as the big black car barged through, forcing the carts to the side of the road and upsetting a youth who attempted a bullfight *pase de pecho* on the Mercedes without descending from his bicycle. Unhurt, he was wildly applauded for this effort, and the driver smiled. It was a lean smile, like a scar, and scarcely altered his expression.

"Look at them," he muttered. "Homeless, on the run, and even worse ahead of them, and they make an excursion of it." He shook his head.

"What did that man say to you?" Barney asked, removing the consul's cigarettes from the glove compartment and offering one to the driver. The latter took two and put them in his pocket.

"He wished him good luck at the frontier," the consul interrupted, sitting forward. "You mustn't bother the driver, Edwin."

"You mean, he *needs* good luck there? Why?"

"Maybe I do," the driver said—and at this point he accelerated so suddenly that the consul was thrown back into the seat—"and maybe I don't."

Barney was certain the man had done this purposely, and his father was clearly of the same opinion, for his neat, mustached mouth was set and hard, and his blue eyes were bright with rage. He stared straight past Barney down the road, unseeing.

They went on in silence to the French frontier. The man drove skillfully and very fast, splitting occasional caravans in two. They ran a gantlet of black, squinted eyes, the car whipping in and out among the carts and scorching the roadsides with hot wind, until at last the final band of refugees appeared ahead, congested at the barrier. These seemed bewildered, stumbling back and forth over flimsy suitcases, clutching papers. The harried officials darted among them, barking like sheep dogs. Then one official saw the Mercedes and started toward it, his manner changing from arrogance to unctuousness as he pushed forward through the peasants.

"Let's have your necktie," the driver said to Barney.

"Why?" Barney said, admiring the assurance of the man, who was not even looking at him. He was watching Consul Sand.

"Give it to him," the consul said. He did not look at Barney either.

The driver put the tie on quickly and with it a lackey's air of self-importance. He faced around to the wheel and clutched it stiffly with both hands as the customs officer came up. "His Excellency, the American Ambassador, and his family," he pronounced in Spanish, looking straight ahead.

The official hesitated. *"Pasaportes?"* he ventured, tentative.

"His Excellency, the American Ambassador, and his family," the driver repeated loudly, as if at a loss to understand what ailed this nincompoop.

"Sí, sí, amigo, pero—"

The driver turned to Consul Sand and touched a finger to an imaginary cap. "It might be sensible, Consul Sand," he said, "to give him a glimpse of that diplomatic passport."

"You know me, do you?" The consul, searching for his passport, spoke in a careful undertone. But the driver did not answer. He shoved the gold-edged passport at the official, who by this time had been cut off from the car by refugees. The official saluted the passport over their heads, then hurled an old woman aside and leaped onto the running board, shouting at the peasants to make way. The Mercedes rolled in triumph to the barrier, where the passport was stamped by a second official. The second official attempted to join the first on the running board, but was dissuaded, and the first escorted them alone to the French side, shouting rather aimlessly now but in a way that infected the French authorities. They were fed up with the refugees, and the Mercedes did honor to their profession. Ignoring the Spaniard, they vied with one another in courtesy and efficiency and saluted with a click of the heels as the Mercedes drew away.

"I'll go with you as far as Perpignan," the driver said. "That's less than an hour from here."

"You honor us," said Consul Sand. His wife, by this time, was exhausted by the tension, but because she was married to a diplomat she adopted a let's-make-the-best-of-it expression that was almost a smile and held her tongue. She had a headache as well as a more immediate predicament, and determined to suffer both in silence. At Perpignan, where this hoodlum would leave them, she could hurry to an inn and there undergo in comfort a ladylike species of collapse.

It was three in the afternoon. Spring had gone north through Roussillon ahead of them, flowering the coastal lowlands and laying a warm haze on the peak of Canigou, which, overlooking Perpignan, was dominant in the distance. Barney Sand, his head out of the window, savored the sweet air and wondered. How swiftly they had left the war behind, the ugliness and want. But no, it had drifted with them, shrouding the presence of the stranger like a smell. And at the outskirts of the town he saw the refugee encampments, like dark, ragged clumps of brush on the green countryside.

The man beside him had been studying the encampment and the faces near the road. "You see, kid," he said, "you can't escape it, no matter how fast or far you go. You can only close your eyes." The words seemed a parting message, for he drew up just inside the town at a garage and removed his coat and knapsack from the car.

"Points, sparkplugs, fuel line, carburetor, battery." The man checked them off on his fingers for a mechanic who had come running out. "Look at all of them for His Excellency, the American Ambassador." His French, like his Spanish, was mangled and mispronounced, but fluent, with the same hard vibrant quality as his English.

Consul Sand was waiting for him as he turned away. "I've seen you before," he said. "Who are you?"

"It'll come to you, Your Excellency. Thanks for the ride."

"I must say you've been very helpful to us," the consul said in a gentle tone, which his son, eavesdropping from the car, knew from long experience to be deceptive.

"Not as helpful as you've been to me," the stranger said.

"No. No, I'm in your debt. I'd like to settle matters if I can. Because," Consul Sand enunciated, "I dislike being in your debt."

"You're not. Among other things, you may have saved me quite a lot of trouble at the border."

"I know that."

"All right, then." The stranger slipped his overcoat through the straps of his pack and shouldered it.

"No, it isn't all right, you see. It might be all right if we were friends. We are not friends." The consul's words were dry ice in the silence, and his tone ensnared the stranger, who had turned away, but now turned back, on the alert. "I despise your methods," the consul told him. "I would have helped you, gun or no gun, even if I remembered you and disliked you as much as you seem to dislike me—because that is my job, as consul. But I did not help you voluntarily, as you helped us."

The stranger studied Consul Sand for several moments.

He seemed unconcerned with the rebuke, as if nothing the consul could do or say was of the slightest interest to him. Yet his eyes held a hint of suspicion, and the grease-streaked hand upon the shoulder strap was clenched tightly in a fist.

"Listen," he said softly, "I'm not interested in your opinions. I'm in a hurry. But what's this song and dance of yours about being in my debt? Just what are you trying to prove? I never helped you voluntarily, I fixed that car for my own good reasons. I took advantage of you, and you know it."

Then the consul smiled. "Yes, I do," he said. "But it's gratifying to hear you admit it." And, bowing slightly from the waist, he turned his back upon the man as if he had never existed.

The stranger remained motionless where he was. He was clearly unwilling to retreat, yet he seemed to know that now he was on unequal footing and could only worsen his position. He glanced at Barney, licking his lips. Then he went away.

"Where are you going?" Barney called.

The man went on down the road to the south, which led back to the refugee encampment. The consul turned to watch him, leaning back on his elbows against the window sill of the car.

"Are you really in his debt?" his son inquired.

"Of course not. I simply wanted to make sure *he* didn't think so," said the consul. "I couldn't stand being beholden to that sort of man." He smiled at his son. "I will say, though, that he had dignity of a kind. He didn't stoop to the parting insult, which is the usual recourse of the loser."

Barney gazed after the stranger. "Maybe he didn't think he was the loser." He could not look his father in the eyes.

The consul winced. "No," he said, "perhaps not. Perhaps he thought it was only the petty revenge of a man who had been made to look ridiculous before his son. And perhaps he was right." In a rare gesture, he patted Barney's shoulder, then walked away toward the garage. There Mrs. Sand, unable to get anybody to pay attention to her, had retired in discreet confusion.

"What do you mean, 'look ridiculous'?" Barney said, uncomfortable. "I mean, you kind of stood up to him when he had that pistol and all."

He went unheard.

Far down the road the stranger was disappearing. In the distance he seemed vulnerable and small, plodding along alone; and in the garage stood the consul, hands in pockets, staring at the floor.

Barney moved out of the way of the mechanic and wandered into the yard of the garage. The new weeds there were brown with exhaust and oil. How strange the day had been, he thought. How strange spring seemed in the gray outskirts of an unfamiliar town.

His mother's voice, dispirited, drifted out from the garage. "You never consider me for a single moment," she was saying to the consul, "but you might at least consider the example you are setting your son."

Barney tossed some small stones at a gas pump in the weeds. He knew to the stone how many times he must jangle the precarious silence before his father would be goaded to the brief skirmish with his son that the latter needed and desired.

"Stop that!" the consul said. "Why don't you go for a walk or something while we're waiting? You're old enough to take care of yourself." He gave him money. "We'll be here for an hour or so," he said.

It was true that Barney could take care of himself, but there lay in him a faint resentment he disdained to acknowledge that his parents offered no companionship. He was not unhappy with them, but he had no brothers or sisters, and the friends in places he had lived, adopted for arbitrary periods, only to be left behind, had never been quite enough. Later, in America, during the war, he was taught how to be selective, but now he took friendship where he found it and made the most of people like the stranger.

I should go after him, he thought; he's got my tie. Set free—or banished—he went off down the road toward the encampment.

Barney waved to an old man seated on a wall. His intimates had often been elders with moments of idleness—doormen, fishermen, derelicts, chauffeurs—and he opened this acquaintanceship by asking the time of day.

But the old man said, in the heavy accent of the South, *"Mais qu'est-ce que ça peut te faire, mon petit, puisque ça change tout le temps?"* He laughed painfully at his own remark, but the effort seemed to tire him, for he took no further notice of the boy who stood beside him.

And Barney, his good-by unnoticed, wandered on.

He paused on the shoulder of the road, observing the encampment. There was a French cavalry officer riding up and down among the refugees, his glitter in sharp contrast to their dusty black. The stranger was there, immobile among the Spaniards. He seemed to be speaking to the officer in their behalf.

Barney slid down an eroded bank and made his way slowly across the field.

The crowd had fallen back, alarmed, and the French officer had reached such a pitch of excitement as to dance his horse in tight, prancing circles around the stranger. His face was crimson, and clearly it was all he could do not to drop the reins and clutch his forehead with both hands. Instead he swung his swagger stick around in short vicious arcs and pointed it in every direction, crying out to the Almighty as he did so. The man on the ground stood calmly, hands in pockets, watching him. He was not quite smiling.

"To the sea!" the French officer shouted. "You have to move down to the sea this instant, or my men will drive you there like so many sheep, do you understand!"

"These people are tired, Your Excellency," the man said in French. "You must allow them a chance to rest a little. And you must see that they get something to eat."

"Eat? Not a bit of it! Not here! To the sea, do you understand, you stupid idiot?" At this point he rode his horse forward at the stranger, who did not flinch. As the horse brushed past him, he removed a vestigial cigarette from his mouth and pressed it to the sweated rump. The horse danced sideways, snorting, and when it came back the officer had his swagger stick raised, and the refugees gasped. The man on the ground did not move. The blow caught him neatly across the side of the face, and he went down. A Spaniard came forward and helped him to his feet, and the officer found himself surrounded. The crowd awaited the struck man's command, but the officer did not. Afraid, and expecting no mercy, he rode roughshod through their ranks, flailing furiously in all directions with his stick, so that women helping children from his path were felled by the blows, and a grandfather, intervening, had his glasses smashed into his eyes. When the officer was in the clear he wheeled his horse, still shouting threats, and cantered gallantly away.

To Barney's surprise the stranger observed this last scene with the same detachment he had demonstrated all that day. Although the blood poured from his opened cheek, he allowed an old woman to mop at it with her black shawl and seemed neither angry nor in pain. The cigarette stump, in fact, still burned in the corner of his mouth, and still he was not quite smiling.

The other men came up and questioned him, and he pointed east in the direction of the coast. They moved away through the crowd, shouting orders. By now a few people had noticed Barney, and a boy not much older than himself came up and asked him for a cigarette.

Barney, moving backward, said he did not smoke.

"*Verdad?*" the boy said. "My little brother smokes." He slipped his hand into Barney's pocket, and Barney struggled free. Then other boys came at him, and he found himself on the ground, a strange hand in each of his pockets and several more attempting to remove his shoes.

The stranger came slowly forward. He spoke roughly to the boys, and all but one of them broke loose. This one had his fingertips on Barney's billfold and could not tear himself away. The man spoke again, and, when the boy only muttered sullenly, reached down and hauled him up by the hair of his head. "*Eh, chico,*" he said, "*bastante, entiende?*"

The boy sat frightened on the ground. "*Sí,*" he said, "*sí, claro, amigo.*"

"*Eso es,*" the man said, and did not look at the boy again. He went on across the field toward the roadway, and Barney followed at a little distance. At the top of the embankment the man turned and waited for him.

"What do you want here, kid?" he asked when Barney came near. "You ought to have more sense than to stick your nose into a place like that." The man waved at the encampment with something like contempt.

"What's the matter with them?" Barney asked. "I thought you liked them."

"Yes, I do, but they're a little desperate right now. You wouldn't know what that means."

They started off together down the road.

"I just came back to get my tie," Barney said, and immediately felt foolish.

"Oh, so that's it. Just a moment." The man was walking very fast, searching impatiently in his pocket for something to stanch the flow of blood

"Also, I guess I kind of wanted to say good-by—I mean, you know, you were with us all day, and I was kind of sorry about that argument a little while ago and all. I mean—Here." And he returned his tie to the stranger, who had ripped it off. "You might as well use it on your face."

The man accepted it without thanks, but glanced appreciatively at Barney. "You're pretty young for your age, but at least you're still honest," he said. He crumpled the tie and held it against his cheek.

Barney said, "Did you leave Spain, too, because of the war?"

"I was in the war, with the Loyalists. Some of us were ordered out of the country."

"You quit? You mean you just deserted them?" Astonished, he moved unconsciously ahead of the man, so that, walking half turned, he might have a better look at him.

"Look, kid, they're beaten. Why go on fighting? There will be other battles, and they won't be lost."

"And those refugees back there," Barney insisted, "what about them?"

The other appeared to guess Barney's implication, for he stopped short. "Yes," he said, "I'm quitting them too. And do you know why, my innocent young friend? Because the French are going to come out here armed to the teeth, and they're going to knock those people around and drive them away like sheep to the coast, the way our hero promised, and if I was there I would come in for some very special treatment—not only because of what I did but because I am what I am, which they would find out, do you see? And I am a very busy man with a lot of work to do. I only went there because I needed a free meal. But I haven't got time to stay and be a martyr."

His tone was so violent that Barney drew back, abashed. "What's the difference between their being at the seacoast and their being here?—that's what I don't see," he mumbled.

"The French don't want a lot of starving people running loose all over the countryside, especially Spaniards. The French have the same contempt for Spaniards that they have for Italians, Germans, Swiss, British—any neighbor, in other words. They want them on the beach with their backs to the water, where they can control them better, that's all—where they can ride up and down with riding crops the way they learned at Saint-Cyr and give the helpless the same punishment they themselves get in every civil-service office in France. I'm prejudiced," he added. "I prefer the Spanish." He peered at the bloody necktie, put his fingers to his face, and winced.

"It's too bad you didn't get that officer," Barney said.

"We'll get him," the man said. "We'll get his name, and we'll get him, sooner or later." He pronounced the "we" with a cold certitude and exclusiveness that in no way included Barney.

They went on in silence.

The day, though ending, was still beautiful, clear in color and quiet and warm. The man glanced at the tie and put it into his pocket.

"Where are you going?" Barney asked.

"West. To the Atlantic coast."

"Oh," Barney said.

He was more and more loath to part with his new friend—and he thought of him already as a friend, though he was not sure whether, much less why, he liked him. And when they came to a traveling carnival, raw-colored, like an infection on the flank of the old town, Barney said as gruffly as possible, "Do you want to fool around in there for a while?"

The man opened his mouth to dismiss the invitation, but at the supplication in the voice of the boy he paused and, after a moment, smiled. Remembering the moment later, Barney was certain that this hard man had been embarrassed.

"All right, Barney," he said. "I'll sit down for a minute, at

least, and have something to drink. Do you have any money?"
The question was asked in a matter-of-fact manner, as if he
had an exactable right to the boy's funds, or to those of anybody else.

"Sure," Barney said. Since he held the purse, he took the
initiative and preceded his friend toward the shooting gallery.

"Squeeze it," the man said after Barney had missed several
times. "Line up your sights, blot it out, and squeeze on your
trigger slowly." A moment later he said, "Barney, you didn't
blot it out. You've got to blot the damned thing out." His tone
was restless, and then he turned away. The boy paid and followed him to a table under the arbor of an inn. "You go
ahead," the man said. "I'll watch you." Sitting there, he
seemed remote to Barney Sand, who longed to enjoy him as
a contemporary.

"The shooting was all I was interested in," Barney told
him, adopting a loud voice and a careless manner. "The rest
is for little kids."

"Is it? I'd try the other things myself if I wasn't so thirsty.
Go ahead."

The boy walked away, glancing back over his shoulder. In
a little while he was back again, unable to conceal his fear that
the man might have left. But his friend had a glass in one
hand, a cigarette in the other; and on the table was a thin cool
bottle of rosé wine.

"This is wonderful," the man murmured. "I appreciate it."
Barney shrugged his shoulders, secretly delighted. He sat down
at the table, and a waiter brought him a glass. Though he
disliked the taste of wine, he got two glasses down and sat
back, lightheaded, in his chair. Across the table, the stranger's
smile was kind, and Barney smiled himself, drank another glass,
and wondered rather dreamily if he was drunk.

What had seemed at first a shabby playground had become
a splendid carnival, its yellowed colors come to life, its hurdy-

gurdy the soul of harmony. In the soft air of the terrace, song-
birds north from Africa and Spain enlivened the new green
leaves, and beyond the cold clear bottle of rosé wine, tinted
magically by the setting sun, the stranger dozed a little, a half-
smile of pleasure on his lips. His creased face, sympathetic in
the strong quality of its ugliness, was commanding even in
repose, and when the dark eyes opened once again to inter-
cept Barney's gaze, the boy glanced too quickly the other way
and said, "This is fine, I'm glad we came here." He found
himself laughing foolishly, and could not stop.

"So am I," the man said. "It's been a long time since I've
had a chance to sit quietly and drink and watch children play
without a thought in their heads. Have you ever had a thought
in your head, my friend? I mean, speaking as the son of His
Excellency, Consul Sand?"

Barney attempted to answer the question literally. He described to the man some thoughts he had on European automobiles. The man nodded, signaling to the waiter for a second
bottle of wine, and then he leaned forward a little and said,
"Tell me about your summers, kid—your vacations, I mean.
Did you ever go to the seashore and fish and sail boats and
things like that?"

"Sure I did, didn't you?"

"No, I didn't. Tell me about it." And he listened carefully.
Barney described to him what it was like at the seashore in
the summertime, exaggerating his adventures to suit the elation of the occasion but presenting nevertheless a clear picture
of childhood summer. ". . . and then sometimes we'd go out
and fish from the sailboat, even, and get all kinds of things
like blackfish and flounder. It was always windy in the after-
noons, and brighter blue, with waves and spray, and sometimes gulls. It was really great, you'd really like it."

"I know I would," the man said; and again, softly to himself, "I know I would."

The tone was wistful, trailing off into regret, and the boy felt abashed and guilty about his own enthusiasm. He observed the man for a moment before he said, "Listen, if you come home some time when I'm there, we could go together. My uncle has a fine little boat, and we could take it out any time we wanted. I mean, I know how to sail and I could show you how, and we could go out off the rocks and swim and maybe fish, and then go for a sail down the coast in the afternoon. Then we could—" But he cut off the excited rush of words, uncertain.

The man was laughing, a quiet, grunting laugh with only a trace of humor in it, and he was shaking his head. "No," he said. "I wish we could," he added, avoiding Barney's vulnerable stare. "And I appreciate the offer, I mean it."

But Barney misunderstood him. "I guess I'm being kind of stupid," he stated. "I mean, I'm still kind of childish, I guess. I only thought—" He stopped, at a loss.

The man was no longer smiling. "No, kid, that's not what I mean," he said. "You live in a different world, that's all." His face relaxed again, and he patted the boy roughly on the shoulder. "You're a nice guy, Barney, damned nice. You just keep going the way you are, and don't let anybody try to change you."

He drank deeply from his glass and refilled it, frowning. Then he looked up again at Barney, with a smile intended to change the subject.

"What do you mean, I live in a different world?" Barney said.

"Look, kid, it doesn't matter, don't take it to heart. I don't even know if I can explain it to you." He drank again, shifting impatiently in his seat. "Forget it."

The boy waited, unrelenting.

"Look," the man said, "you live in a different world, that's all. Your family has money, sailboats, the whole business. They

don't want anything to change except taxation. Neither will
you. You'll accept the status quo, adapt yourself to it, even
exploit it. But you won't want to change anything. That's the
difference between your world and the real world, where
everything needs changing."

"You mean you think I—"

"Look, Barney, I'm not talking about you, I'm talking about
your situation. It's just different, that's all. It's small and selfish, and it's dying," the man said harshly, "but you don't know
that, and it's not your fault. It's the way you were brought up.
You were trained not to know, not to see. Take those refugees
this morning. You've already half forgotten them, haven't you?
I mean, the difference between them with their wheelbarrows
and you with your Mercedes-Benz?"

Barney stared at him, dismayed. "No, I—"

"Haven't you?"

"Yes."

"Listen, kid, you're still honest, so try to understand me.
The great majority of the people in the world are allowed to
live like dogs. But the world is changing, and it's going to
change much more. The sooner you realize this, the better.
It's part of history, and it's taking place right now. In the past
thirty years, in Russia and China and now in Spain, we've
fought only the first battles. The true war, the Great Twentieth-Century War, will go on and on and on until it's won,
even though few people recognize that it exists and even less
know what it means."

The man was excited now, his big hands, palms up, tense-
fingered, moving in heavy circles about the table, his big voice
grating. "This war," he proclaimed oratorically, angrily, "will
have many phases and many names and will be waged in terms
of politics and nations, imperialism and nationalism, but it is
only the final war of economics between the many and the

few, between a new society of human welfare and the old society of dog-eat-dog."

He glared at Barney, then dismissed him cruelly with a wave of his hand. "Perhaps you can't understand, not yet," the voice concluded, "but your father and people like him represent the few. These few control the money and the churches and the armies, and they are powerful." He paused to lick his lower lip, a habit with him. "But we represent the many," he said softly, "and we are going to win."

Barney sat stiffly in his seat, struck dumb by the man's intensity, which hung in the sudden silence like some explosive gas. He had to bite the insides of his cheeks to keep from laughing, as he had so often in school and at funerals and in church. There was something ridiculous here, a speech like this could not have been meant for *him*—yet the words inspired him, excited him, and for the first time in his life he felt a sense of direction, of participation in important affairs. He wanted to rush forth and do battle, though with what he could not have said, unless it was the passive existence he had lived to date. And he was intrigued by the possibility that his way of life, however innocent, was built on selfishness and wrong.

For Barney had never questioned the nature of his right to the swimming and the fishing, the boats and the blue summers, which he had described so confidently to the stranger. His ignorance of human misery had been consigned to him with as much loving care as an inheritance. His parents recognized the misery, or sniffed it on the wind, at least, like some sort of embarrassing smell, and made amends through consideration of servants, contributions to charity, and, as death edged closer, increasingly fervent attendance at church. His mother might say with a sigh, "You just don't know how lucky you are to have everything you have, when there are Arme-

nians and things who'd give their eyeteeth for that snow pud-
ding." But the year before when, hard on the heels of puberty,
he had suffered a first attack of liberalism and exposed to his
father the unfair distinctions between himself and his best
friend, the chauffeur's son—distinctions made by everyone in
the household, but most determinedly by the chauffeur—Consul Sand had retorted, "What you don't yet realize, young
man, is that people are where they are because of what they
are; you can't help people who can't help themselves. Why,
even if that infernal Party was to divide everything equally
among everybody, the status quo would be restored within ten
years! Ten years!" he had repeated, rattling his newspaper.

Such notions as these, before the flight from Spain, the
consul had managed to pass intact to his son. But afterward
his task became far more complicated. He felt forced at times
to take refuge in the implication that, as a member of the
foreign service, he had access to secret intelligence which
would bring the boy to his senses immediately if divulged. He
would refer to dark statistics of slavery and salt mines, and was
wont to conclude with an observation on the meaning of democracy. In doing so, he was making a serious error, for it had
not occurred to his son to support the Party or to question
democracy, he was simply curious about the difference.

Barney never forgot the expressions of the two men, face
to face over the table. He could not identify his own reaction,
but it had expressed itself in a vague embarrassment for his
father unrelated to the normal embarrassment of a child for
its parent. Consul Sand had appeared quite suddenly at the
carnival and, nodding curtly at the stranger, had laid a pos-
sessive hand on his son's shoulder.

"Isn't this an odd hour for you to be drinking wine?" he
remarked. "Come along; we have to go."

"I haven't done anything wrong," Barney said. The quick
dark of April stole across the carnival grounds and sank beside

them. "Wine is a food, Your Excellency." He grinned at his drinking companion, who looked the consul in the face and laughed.

"Come along," the consul repeated. His tone, though mild, foretold a private reckoning for the boy's impertinence. And he stared questioningly at the other man, who stood up now and said, "He drank the wine to be polite, Your Excellency. You should count yourself lucky that your son turned out so well."

Consul Sand stiffened at his inflection. "You ought to know better than to drink with a child this age. What the devil are you doing with him, anyway?" he exclaimed in a sudden access of irritation.

"I'm not a child. And I invited him to come here with me," the boy interrupted. "He saved me from getting everything stolen off me—"

"*From* me," his father said. "Then you've put me in his debt again." He turned to the stranger. "You're Jacobi, aren't you? You wore a beard last time I saw you."

"I'd been in action. I was unshaven. There's a difference."

"I recognize it. And you came to see me. You were with the Jefferson Battalion."

"Yes. You refused to help us, Mr. Sand." Jacobi's tone was muted, but its note of quiet anger made the boy look up. He saw no longer the stranger's peaceful face, but a pair of thin, hard, heavy-lidded eyes under thick black hair. The face was sallow, with high cheekbones and a protruding mouth, and the nose was badly broken. His father's face was strangely delicate by comparison. Yet it too was strong, and there was a stubborn set to it that he had never before noticed.

"Yes, I did," Consul Sand was saying. "You did not represent our country, Mr. Jacobi, but the International Party."

"That may be. But the Battalion represented our country, Mr. Sand, which I prefer to think your attitude did not."

"You're mistaken, sir. My attitude *did* represent our country, whatever my own feelings in the matter." Consul Sand spoke evenly, reflectively. "We could only regard the Jefferson Battalion as a group of soldiers of fortune under foreign supervision."

"Not soldiers of fortune, Mr. Sand, but partisans."

"No doubt. But in my way, perhaps, I am a partisan too, Mr. Jacobi. There are other causes besides your own."

In the long moment that the two men stood gauging each other Barney remained seated between them, enthralled. His father's hand still rested on his shoulder, but Jacobi's hand lay lightly on Barney's wineglass, as if to protect this symbol of their friendship from Consul Sand.

Then Jacobi broke the silence. "That is not a matter we can settle here," he said, and yawned. "I detained you because your son offered to pay my way." He nodded at the bottle of wine. "That's the second," he said. He eyed the other man expectantly.

Consul Sand drew a bill from his pocket. He laid it gently on the table, disdaining the contemptuous toss which his son perceived that Jacobi had expected. The latter called the serving girl. "I didn't ask for a tip," he said. "She'll get your change."

"Thank you," said Consul Sand and smiled.

The boy gave his hand to Jacobi. "Good-by," he said. He felt dizzy from wine and could not see very well.

"Good-by," Jacobi said. "Thanks very much."

"Will I see you again?"

"If you do, just say it's Barney Sand, and I'll remember."

"Maybe we can go sailing someday, and fishing." He said this with such enthusiasm that his father glanced at him, and Jacobi laughed outright.

"I hope so," Jacobi said. He hesitated before adding, "If

His Excellency is sure enough of your affection and respect to allow a bad influence like me into his house."

Consul Sand, who had started away, turned quickly to face him and said, "Because apparently you have helped my son, Mr. Jacobi, I am in your debt, and you would be welcome in my house. But I would like to say that, were our positions reversed, and were this your young son standing here, I would not need so badly to win my point as to try to degrade you in his presence."

Jacobi's weathered face changed color. He sat down heavily, not looking at them further, and poured himself another glass of wine. He was still sitting there in the gathering dark when Barney, confused, turned the corner with his father.

3

"Alex. Who's this Alex?" Sand asked when the editor returned from the telephone. They were alone in the café with one waiter, who stood at the dew-streaked window, leaning on a mop.

"One of my contacts. A dirty little man. One of the million dirty little men who infest all Europe these days and make things so much easier for the rest of us." The editor produced a pad and made some quick notes on his call.

"What makes you think you can trust him?"

"I trust him the way I trust a good money-changer. He has a steady clientele, and he makes so much money that he can't afford to cheat." The editor's cynicism, an occupational ailment, was qualified by a round red face, a face that was earnest despite an uneasy smile. Stranded by the surf of life, he was entrenched in a sand castle of common sense, and presumed to analyze the sea on the basis of his damp bathing suit. "Listen," he was saying now, "it was simply a matter of time before this happened."

"You're pretty sure of that, are you?" Sand liked this man and simultaneously deplored him.

"Of course! Look at the record—" The editor, rapping on

his pad with the eraser of his pencil, delivered himself of the legend of Jacobi. Most of it was long since familiar to Sand. It was based on little specific information, since few people knew Jacobi well. He had been born in some dark, suspicious region of Central Europe. He had come to America as a boy, been educated there, and had become a citizen and an editor of the Party newspaper. The Party was fashionable in the early thirties and, for other nations at least, considered salutary. And he had been a Loyalist volunteer in Spain. Sand had sought out his name in a book about the Spanish Civil War—a "fearless, brilliant leader," it had called him. But at mid-century, in a book about the Party, the same correspondent referred to the Jacobi of that period as a "murderous hireling of the Party," which by that time had suffered a severe decline in public esteem.

In World War II, however, Jacobi had been a hero. His exploits as liaison man between Allied Intelligence and the underground guerrillas of Southern Europe had won him extravagant praise from reputable people. These were later to regret their shortsightedness. They had failed to perceive that, far from being a hero, Jacobi had been a dangerous subversive, a menace to church and state. It appeared, indeed, that he had risked his life unpatriotically, having shared his information with a certain ex-Ally. And finally his name was linked with an espionage ring about to be investigated. He proved his guilt to everyone's satisfaction by renouncing the country. "If flag-waving is what my citizenship now requires of me, if freedom of speech is now an empty phrase, then I am glad to go. I love my country, but I cannot accept 'my country, right or wrong,'" he told reporters at the boat.

"Which is all very well," the editor interrupted himself, "except for the fact that he did not leave voluntarily. He was thrown out."

"How could they throw him out?" Sand demanded. "He's a naturalized citizen, goddam it, and a naturalized citizen has every right that we have."

"Legally, perhaps. But in practice ex-aliens are vulnerable. Usually some technicality is enough—something they did prior to full citizenship, or even some mistake in their entrance or citizenship papers."

"Listen, Jacobi came to America as a child. He couldn't have filled out his own papers, much less commit a crime."

"If you'll just relax a minute, Barney, my lad, I'll let you in on a little secret, and I want you to keep it quiet, because it's a necessary evil that none of us can be too proud of." He paused. "They had nothing on Jacobi in that espionage case, so they decided to deport him as next best thing. But, as you've guessed, his citizenship was relatively invulnerable. So, according to a government man I know, they checked on his parents until they found some discrepancy in the father's papers. The father doesn't speak the language and has no money and is pretty vulnerable. They pointed this out to Jacobi, then suggested that he might prefer to leave the country rather than have his government go to all the expense and trouble of deporting him. He left the country. In other words, he was thrown out."

"Is that true?"

"Yes, that's true. And don't look at me that way; I didn't do it."

"And it doesn't make you mad." Somewhere along the way, Sand thought, you turned in your integrity for an extra baked potato.

"No, I'm afraid it doesn't," the editor said. "Look, Barney, I'm a liberal myself, always have been, but we're fighting for survival these days, we can't fuss over our methods! Face the facts! Except for public consumption, at home and abroad, your kind of honor is out of date."

"Good God Almighty!" Sand exclaimed, disgusted.

"Look, do you really want to know about Jacobi or are you just here to read me the Bill of Rights? So you want to learn the facts of life the hard way, but remember, you're still working for me. I don't have to sit here and—" He stopped, mistaking Sand's silence for subservience. "All right, then. So, anyway, Jacobi came to Europe. He disappeared for several years into the Eastern countries. Then he came to Paris on a Party tour and remained as a Party figurehead. But he was too powerful to remain a figurehead," the editor remarked. "He became restless, took part in things. They couldn't control him, and so—" He ground an inky thumb on the café table.

"How do you know?"

"I don't *know* this, of course," the editor demurred, "and we'll have to report the expulsion as a rumor. But he'll be eliminated."

"I see," Sand said, restraining a temptation to salute. "And therefore you would not bother to assign a man to find him, find the truth?"

"You, for instance?"

"Well, now that you mention it—"

The editor winced, peering carefully at Sand as if to perceive some hidden illness. But he saw only the self-contained young man whose innocent face, with its odd hint of private humor, had become, like the calendar, a feature of the office, and like the calendar was referred to in need but seldom noticed. The editor shook his head with slow, sardonic emphasis, and his mouth formed a small inaudible "No."

And then Sand remarked that he had once met Jacobi and spent a day with him. The editor, startled, raised his eyes again, and this time his expression read, "You continue to astonish me, Sand, I am almost tempted to ask you how that came about." But he withheld the question, as Sand had surmised, because in posing it he would cede to a subordinate the initiative in a weighty conversation.

And finally Sand said that he planned to seek out Jacobi in any case, and volunteered his resignation. Because the decision had just come to him, and because he was delighted with it, his tone was pleasant. There was nothing stubborn about it, only a quiet certainty. He went on to suggest that, in exchange for accreditation, he would promise any story to the wire service.

"You feel accreditation will make all the difference, then. You imagine they'll carry you to Jacobi on their shoulders when they realize you represent an American wire service!"

"No," Sand said. "To be quite honest with you, the accreditation will only make me feel less irresponsible."

The editor slapped his palm to his forehead before he could collect himself. And then he said, "You haven't a chance—you know that, don't you?—not one chance in a thousand."

"That one chance is worth while, isn't it, for a story like this? And you can get along without me at the office."

"I certainly can. After this, especially. Listen!" he shouted suddenly, forgetting the presence of the waiter, "the Party hasn't hidden Jacobi just for the hell of it! And they won't play games with you, Sand, they mean business!"

The waiter glanced up at the mention of Jacobi, and, to Sand's relief, wandered over to their table. Bored, he was only anxious to contribute an opinion of his own. "*Ce Jacobi, hein?*" he said, nodding his head, as if this remark in itself had been profound. "*C'est un héros, celui-là—de deux guerres.*" He slapped his hand on a folded bicep. "*C'est un américain,*" he admitted, "*mais tout de même c'est un homme du peuple.*" He eyed them darkly, rearranging their coffee cups on the table. He was a restless man, disgruntled, who probably drank more than was good for the longevity of his job.

Sand nodded for the waiter's benefit but also in agreement

with his editor's remark. Later he wondered about that nod, since he had given the Party's methods little thought. It occurred to him, for example, that he would not like to find himself at the mercy of that waiter. Yet his excitement diverted his mind from danger as the effort of living diverts the mind from death, and he felt, quite unreasonably, that he *had* to succeed, if only to demonstrate something still undefinable but of the greatest importance to the survival of his code.

"I'd just like to know the truth about Jacobi," he remarked. "Why he thinks the way he does, and how that thinking has gotten him into trouble."

"You sound like an old-fashioned crusading reporter, Sand," the editor said. His yawn was sour and constructed, and it hinted that Sand's idea, however harebrained, had forced him to evaluate what he himself had settled for. "You're behind the times. People don't care about the truth these days, they want the facts—or, better yet, an interpretation of the facts by somebody whose point of view is comforting to their own. So why risk your neck for nothing? The hero of one generation is the damned fool of the next."

Sand shifted impatiently in his chair. Perhaps he *was* attempting the impossible, but in the end the clearly possible was so often disappointing. He wanted to believe that nothing was impossible, in the way one believes one will never grow old.

He was aware that, having known Jacobi, his chances might be better than those of other Western journalists, but he was at an equal disadvantage when it came to locating the man in the first place. Once this obstacle was overcome, he told himself, the rest was a matter of resourcefulness. He spoke good French, and he knew Paris, and he was, as the editor remarked with a shake of the head in parting, quite harmless in appearance. Sand was slight and fair and agreeably plain, with curious, wide, blinking eyes and a chronic expression of surprise that often corresponded with his condition. Insofar as it suggested a total absence of guile, the expression was an asset, but it could not offset the disadvantage he bore with him from the very first moment of his search. This disadvantage was the simple exercise of his own candor.

But later, walking, almost trotting, in the clear September sun of the Faubourg Saint-Honoré, he looked deceptively like a young man with a future embarking upon some spirited but altogether reasonable quest, and not at all as he saw himself, a fool breasting a heavy surf for the pure hell of it.

He walked rapidly, working away a nervous energy, but near the corner of his street apprehension overtook him. The many-faced motley buildings sat in watch, evoking dim continental treacheries, intrigue—and he started, drawing back from a foreboding. He cursed himself and rounded the corner, whistling. At his apartment he took a soiled card from his billfold and studied the telephone number of a man he did not trust named Rudi Gleize.

4

Rudi's card read "MONSIEUR RUDOLF," with a telephone number but no address. The card was three years old, and its aspect of cheap impermanence sharpened Sand's misgivings about approaching Rudi in the first place. But it's hardly likely, he told himself irrationally, that the number is still valid. He laid the card down on the table by the telephone.

Dialing, he pictured the cheerless bistro in which the ring would sound, for men like Rudi never had a telephone at home, in the rare instances when they had true homes at all. They were always reached through some café crouched on the final corner of some empty street, where the band of regulars, men and women of obscure hours and incomes, nursed one thin wine while awaiting dim salvations. He could even imagine the *patronne* who answered, a pale ex-prostitute with an endless cigarette, a cat, a red coiffure, and huge, goodhearted cynicism. "Monsieur Rudolf? *Pas ici, monsieur. . . . Dites-donc, on ne sait jamais, cher monsieur, ils passent parfois, ces types, c'est tout. . . . B'en, oui, d'accord. . . . Comment? . . . Monsieur— Sahnd? Et votre numéro? . . . Entendu, monsieur. . . . Mais je vous en prie, monsieur . . .*"

Despite her vagueness about Rudi, adopted to protect them both in any skirmish with the police, Sand guessed that

Rudi would have the message within minutes. And indeed, his telephone rang within half an hour. The woman announced that Monsieur Rudolf would join Monsieur Sand at the Georges V bar in forty minutes.

It was so typical of Rudi and his mysteries, Sand thought, to have the woman telephone. Walking up the avenue toward their rendezvous, he suffered another surge of doubt, like a man carrying home an impulsive purchase that he secretly suspects he may not really want at all.

Rudi Gleize was more to Sand than an odd acquaintance. He represented the labyrinth beneath the desolate scene of postwar Europe, a demimonde of that murky intrigue which shrouded the streets of the continental capitals with the damp breath of a ground fog. Not all the denizens of this world were criminals in the professional sense, although there were numbers of these. Many more were stateless persons, aimless and unattached, whose one allegiance was to survival. Others were agents of the numerous underground networks, vending their patriotism for pay. But most were the average people of normal times who lacked the fiber to make a fresh start, whose cynical despair about the future of Europe was the excuse for seizing its remains. There were the opportunists and the looters, young people for the most part, but ageless in their outlook, whose ranks included Rudi Gleize and a woman he called Sara.

Sand had crossed their paths in 1948, in Prague. In the spring of that year he had graduated from college and, still uncertain as to his future, had gone to Europe for the summer with a friend. But when September came and the friend had gone, Sand found himself staying on in Paris. He was delighted there as he had never been before—with the art galleries, cafés, excursions to Senlis, Chantilly, Fontainebleau; with red burgundy and *quenelles de brochet* and a handsome French lady of good family and unhappy marriage who was at

home to him in a large Louis XV apartment on the Place
François Ier; and, for all these reasons, with himself. When his
mistress departed for Cannes he knew and enjoyed that peculiar Paris melancholy—he was reading Chateaubriand at the
time—and when she did not return he set off in October for
Vienna, and from there, impulsively, to Prague, timing his ar-
rival with the thirtieth anniversary of the Republic. The Republic had been for several months a dominion of the Party,
and he went there, among other reasons, to witness Jacobi's
theories in action.

Prague fascinated and oppressed him. It retained a dark
medievalism which had its most striking expression in the
bridges over the Moldau and the stark statue silhouettes that
rose against the opposite bank and the bleak Hradcany Castle
on the hill beyond. The city was charcoal in the way that Paris
was warm gray, and the lean air of late October warned of
winter, which, as in some legend of the North, was depthless
and might never end.

Here, in this atmosphere of unreality and change, Sand
had wandered into the underworld of Rudi Gleize. He had
heard in Vienna that Prague black marketeers were penalized
by hanging, and he had small hope of coming across these
transient creatures during his stay. Nevertheless, on his very
first day, at lunch, he discovered a note wrapped in his napkin
with the bread: "Will exchange kroner for dollars. Careful,
please"; and glanced up to see a terrified waiter watching the
doors of the empty restaurant. Nervous, he wrote on the back
of the note, "How much?" and held a twenty-dollar travelers
check in his lap as the waiter approached. The man pretended
not to see it. He came back after a little while with a roll of
bills wrapped in another napkin, which replaced the original
on the table after an elaborate series of alarums and flourishes,
during which the check was whisked into his pocket. Sand,
counting the kroner later, discovered that he had received four

hundred to the dollar as opposed to the legal rate of fifty, and
it was in an attempt to spend his twenty dollars in one week
that he came to know Rudi Gleize.

He had been to a propaganda film that conveyed the on-
looker around a typical American city of canine beauty parlors
and Negro tenements, and afterward to a very fine concert of
Smetana's "Má Vlast," in honor of the Republic's anniversary,
and felt much in need of less momentous entertainment. He
came upon a dance hall called, mysteriously, the 5P, and stood,
quite lonely, at its bar. There, toward the end of his second
slivovich, the doors opened and an entrance was made that he
was to see often repeated.

The man was sleek and neatly dressed in a black suit and
tie, and he threw a black topcoat to an attendant without any
change of expression whatsoever. He had straight black hair
and a full face, curiously soft and unidentifiable as to race or
age, which Sand identified, astonished, as that of his waiter at
lunch. The man came forward, and a place was made for him
at the bar. He did not appear to recognize Sand, but stood
immobile, observing the dance floor.

Sand needed badly to talk to somebody, but the counte-
nance of this fleshy Cinderella discouraged an approach. Then
he found himself accosted by a drunken man of middle age
who wanted to know, in German and in feeble English, why
Sand was wearing a red waistcoat. The man was belligerent,
interrupting Sand's response with the observation that Sand
was an impostor. He had a curious emblem in his buttonhole
that he fingered constantly, like a sore.

Sand said that he did not understand, to which the stranger
retorted that he was not only an impostor but a spy. "I hate
you," the gentleman remarked.

"Do you really? Why?"

"I despise you," the gentleman continued. "Not only this,
I do not trust you."

"And whom do you trust?" Sand asked, his caution suc-
cumbing to the *slivovich*. "Your new leaders, perhaps?"

The gentleman reflected for a moment. "I do not trust
anybody," he decided, "except myself." He tapped himself
significantly on the temple. "And even this one," he added
sadly, "I do not trust, not always." He moved slowly across the
room, and the other people at the bar stared at Sand with a
variety of expressions.

Then he felt a hand on his sleeve and turned to see the
man in black, who gave him a warning glance. The latter left
the bar, glancing back over his shoulder, and Sand followed
him out onto the shuttered streets.

"You are being foolish." The man took his arm as they
edged along the sidewalk. "We do not play games in this city
any more."

"So you speak English," Sand said slowly. "Didn't I see
you earlier today? Why didn't you speak it then?"

"Don't be sil-ly," the man said. As Sand was to learn, this
was one of his favorite phrases, and he did not say it in a casual
manner but with enunciated scorn. They moved in silence
into Wenceslas Square, where the huge portraits of the leaders
loomed out of the darkness, in readiness for the next day's
Anniversary Parade. His companion showed no inclination to
leave him, and Sand, ill at ease, inquired about the drunken
man in the bar.

"The one with the emblem in his buttonhole—you noticed it?—was one of our best cinema directors. He is still a
cinema director, for them—" He gestured at the posters without facial comment. "We call them the 'in-the-buttonholes,'
people like that."

"And those others in there?"

"Collaborators also, for the most part. A few patriots. There
are less and less each day."

"You seem to know about everybody."

"I do, yes—everybody who matters. That is my business."

"Your business? And money-changing?"

"Please speak more carefully. Yes, that is my business too. Name any business within reason, that is my business too."

"You are even a waiter, then."

The other smiled. "No, that I am not. Only upon occasion, like today. You see, I have a friend who tells me when the tourists come to the restaurant. And all tourists go to that restaurant because the owner is an in-the-buttonhole and the hotel people must recommend it. It is a very bad restaurant."

"At any rate, I made a lot of money."

"Yes, you did. But you did not make as much as myself, I am afraid. The next time you will purchase an airline ticket to Brussels—they are in great demand these days—and for that I will give you five hundred kroner for your dollar. Meanwhile, if there is anything you wish to see, or anyone you wish to meet, please consider me at your disposal." At Sand's expression, he smiled again, saying, "Yes, I am an influential man. My father knew the late President; but it is not that. There are many kinds of influence."

"You are one of them, then?" Sand remarked, displeased.

"Don't be sil-ly. I am neither on one side nor the other. I am simply a little man named Rudolf Gleize—little Rudi, that is all I am." He held out his hand.

"My name is Sand," Sand told him.

"I know it is," Rudi said. "I am honored. And I would like to see you again."

"I'm sure you would," Sand said, and laughed.

"No, no, no, I am serious. I like you. I don't need your business, although it is useful. I like to talk to you, it is very simple. I was with the British in the war, you see, and I like to practice English. So I will see you?"

"Of course, if you like."

"Good." Rudi performed a little bow. "Good night, my

dear Sand." He slipped away along the buildings before Sand could ask him where they were to meet again and when, a quick, portly man alone in the dead streets of early morning beneath the gray-white posters and the garish red-and-yellow lamp posts.

The following day Sand walked in the Anniversary Parade, marching up the long incline of the square with detachments of warlike waiters and martial shopgirls. Along the rooftops, bent by the November wind, small figures moved back and forth, their submachine guns silhouetted against the sky. Police were everywhere. The marchers were halted at the summit of the hill, beneath the balconies of the city library, where they were harangued by the new President. His voice was amplified across the city by huge loudspeakers, and during his pauses the flapping of the mighty posters could be heard. A claque beneath the speaker's balcony cheered wildly at appointed intervals, but the noise barely carried to the first ranks of the citizens before it scattered, with the autumn leaves, across the empty silence of the square.

"There is still some resistance, they haven't consolidated as yet, you understand," Rudi explained to Sand later, going to the door and opening it suddenly to make certain nobody was listening. The theatrical gesture, as Sand was to learn, was typical of Rudi, who had been present in Sand's hotel room when he returned from the parade. Sand did not bother to ask an explanation but let himself be taken in hand entirely by this man, his self-appointed guide to this new world. And indeed, Rudi escorted him everywhere, even as far as Karlovy Vary, where they purchased Bohemian crystal and lived exclusively, it seemed to Sand, on fine white wines and caviar. And on his final evening in Prague, Rudi joined him once more at the cabaret. He entered a few minutes after Sand and observed him from the bar.

Sand was dancing with a hostess named Eva, a languid

red-haired girl who did her utmost to seduce him then and there. The girl was very drunk, and to Sand's alarm kept gesturing at a political mural on the wall and crying out, "Big stuff, hey? Big stuff!" in heavy English. It was the only English she knew, but the derision in her tone was unmistakable. A man came out onto the floor and signaled to her, and when she left, no longer giggling, Sand went to Rudi at the bar.

"Don't dance with those girls," Rudi hissed at him. "They work with the police."

Sand turned to look at them, and found a number of them watching him. "Which ones?" he asked.

Rudi nodded toward three or four of the prettier ones.

"How about the one I was dancing with? Do you know about her? She was laughing at that mural."

Rudi nodded, and whispered after a moment, "It doesn't matter what she believes herself, the pay is very good. These days one cannot afford to believe too strongly about anything."

"In other words, you think she *is* one."

"Yes," Rudi said. "She is one." He seemed upset, staring fixedly at the girl and at the man who had summoned her.

A short time later he signaled covertly to Sand, and they left the cabaret. "I have business tonight," Rudi said. "I have to leave you." He took Sand's Paris address and shook him warmly by the hand. "I know you don't think much of me," he said, "but I was a gentleman once, and perhaps when you see me next I will be a gentleman again." Beneath the old black Borsalino hat his boyish face relaxed into a smile that was almost shy, and then he turned and hurried off into the darkness.

Rudi Gleize appeared in Paris early in 1949. He could not speak freely over the telephone, he said, but he wanted Sand to meet his wife. It was clear that he wanted something more than that, especially since Sand had never heard about the wife until that moment. Rudi said that he was stopping at the Hotel Victoire and would meet Sand in the Café de la Paix.

Rudi's appearance, a soiled shirt notwithstanding, was as opulent as ever. He looked harried, however, as if at any moment he might spring from his seat and flee. His story was fantastic, but so many true accounts were fantastic at the time that it seemed plausible enough.

His wife, he said—and he did not trouble himself with any more explanation of this new phenomenon than a slight pause in which he glanced at Sand—his wife had been indiscreet, and he had been forced to get her out of the country immediately. Then he himself had managed to get on a plane, but at Brussels he was met, not by his thankful wife, but by a delegation from his embassy, which attempted to claim him at customs. He was an escaped criminal, they said, with an invalid passport, and they demanded custody of him. The Belgian officials took his passport but awarded him temporary political asylum until the matter could be clarified. Not knowing how temporary this asylum might be, he had fled with his wife to the frontier, where, under the guidance of a refugee friend, they had entered Marcel's Café in the border village of D——, passed through its kitchen, its back yard, and its enormous, filthy chickencoop, and emerged in a cabbage patch in France.

Rudi's account of the passage through the chickencoop, clutching two suitcases as the startled fowl caromed against his head and shoulders, defecating wildly onto the neat black suit, was grotesquely amusing to Sand. He had a clear picture of the two fugitives, stumbling unglamorously forward against the onslaught of guano and feathers. But Rudı was not amused.

"The crossing cost me a fortune," he said, grimacing. "And now we are here in the Hotel Victoire, without a cent and without papers. I am going to beg you to give us our first meal in two days."

Sand nodded. "But why the Hotel Victoire," he asked, "if you haven't got a cent?"

And Rudi said, "Don't be sil-ly. What does it matter where one stays if one has no money at all? One may as well be comfortable. And the people in the little places are much more anxious about money, and about identification too. But here we can bluff for a little while." He shrugged his shoulders.

Sara joined them in a short time. "You know Sara?" Rudi asked, smiling a little. Sand, rising, said he did not, but saw immediately that he was mistaken, for Sara was the Eva of the cabaret in Prague. She acknowledged his recognition with a nod, then allowed herself to be formally introduced as Sara Gleize. The understanding that the past had no relation to present circumstances was implicit in the introduction.

Eventually, through an arrangement so complex, and involving so many heretofore unmentioned individuals of Rudi's acquaintance, that Sand never approached its inner mysteries, the Gleizes came to terms with the Hotel Victoire, and, with an attitude of good riddance on both sides, repaired to a converted brothel in the rue Caumartin, near the Trinité Church. Here an elderly refugee gave soup and shelter to his displaced countrymen.

At first they moved rarely from this lost labyrinth of mirrors and vulgar murals. Sand would see them from time to time, but gradually lost sight of them. As a special student in the Ecole des Sciences Politiques, he was absorbed and very busy. He was aware, however, before his departure the next summer for America, that Rudi was enmeshed in strange business affairs of many kinds, and was still arranging for British passports through the Hungarian agent of a small Swiss printing establishment in Tangier. Rudi had given him a card with a telephone number and the inscription, "MONSIEUR RUDOLF," should Sand ever interest himself in business. At this time he had been, for several weeks, a citizen of Egypt.

Sand chose a table in the corner from which he could observe the other clients. The bar had been recommended to him once as a place to observe international crime, and there were indeed some curious specimens. To Sand they looked less like human beings than like satyrs, too exalted in their evil to share his own qualities, or even his failings. They had a distinct other-world air about them, these people, a hard patina that had covered them over like a shell, enclosing forever the softness, the pathos, of humankind. He supposed it was power that transformed them, power beyond all recrimination; for petty criminals, however vicious, were far too ruffled by the winds of law to permit this ice to form, and retained their human qualities, while these did not.

Rudi Gleize was in the process of metamorphosis, Sand thought. But to all appearances, as he entered the bar, he was already as crystallized as any man there. He wore the black suit and the black tie, and his face was as well fed and ageless as ever. The signs of the change were the replacement of the old black Borsalino with a Homburg hat and the manner in which the hat was dangled with cool importance from one finger. Sand studied the entrance, fascinated—the alert face of the barman, the hush in a nearby conversation, the general attention Rudi Gleize demanded and received. And he held his seat, for he knew that Rudi had already noticed him. Rudi was speaking softly to one of several men who had drifted like sharks into his area. Then Rudi grimaced, twirled his Homburg up onto his wrist, and made his way between the tables in the direction of Sand. He had arrived and seated himself before Sand could regain his composure, before a word was spoken between them.

"Well, well," Rudi said, turning to him. "So you are back.

What a happy surprise, my excellent friend. How are you?"
He proffered a quick hand and an elaborate smile, behind
which lurked affection in scattered traces about the eyes.

Sand said he was fine, and asked after Sara. Sara was also
fine, it seemed, but the subject was quickly changed by Rudi
to one Sand sensed was closer to his heart. "What brings you
here?" Rudi asked, and it was plain that he expected an answer that would eventually involve himself. While Sand explained, Rudi observed the comings and goings in the bar with
the aid of the mirrors on the walls. "You remember our little
business in Praha," he interrupted, "and the Bohemian crystal
you brought back with you?" Rudi sighed. "A nice profit you
made, yes? There are so many nice little businesses like that."
He shook his head. It was clear that their reunion did not
interest him, and he put his hands on the table edge, prepa-
ratory to getting to his feet.

"As a matter of fact, I have a favor to ask of you, Rudi."

"A favor?" Rudi glanced warily at Sand, then signaled to
the waiter and ordered a vermouth cassis.

Sand shifted in his chair. "I thought perhaps you could
help me, Rudi."

"If it is possible. Of course."

"Do you know of a man named Jacobi?"

Rudi gazed at him, alert for the first time in their conversation. "Of course," he repeated.

"It's said he's in disgrace with the Party, that they have
expelled him and are keeping him in hiding here in Paris. If
this could be verified in some way, it would be valuable in
formation." Sand hesitated.

Rudi pursed his olive lips. "Naturally," he said.

"Especially to a reporter," Sand said. He went on to explain that he had known Jacobi and about his hopes for an
interview. "What do you think my chances are?"

"What are the chances of a fish in a desert?" Rudi said,

"Don't be sil-ly, my poor Sand." He took up his gloves and his Homburg and straightened in his chair.

"All right," Sand said. "But I am going to try. And if you will help me, I will share my valuable information with you."

"I already possess your valuable information," Rudi murmured. "In fact, I have already sold it." Nevertheless, he leaned back again as if he were thinking about something else.

"Then it's true about Jacobi—the disgrace, I mean?"

Rudi made an abrupt gesture with his hand. "Oh yes, it is true, but my knowledge does not help you, my friend. Your wire service will require more proof than my—ah—customers require of me." He paused. "However, I will help you because once you gave help to me, and because you are my friend I will help you too." He replaced the gloves on the table and turned to Sand with a sudden smile. "What is it you imagine I can do for you?"

"You can introduce me to members of the Party who might be of use."

Rudi shrugged his shoulders, but he did not ask the question Sand had already put to himself and beyond which he was unable to see a solution: "And then?" And Sand took hope from Rudi's silence, sensing that Rudi had already perceived a means to the end which he, Sand, could not have imagined and indeed might never know at all. He waited.

Rudi took a series of delicate sips from his apéritif. "And if," he said at last, "you should happen to find Jacobi, you will of course let me know immediately, before anybody else, where he is?"

His tone made Sand uneasy, and he too paused before he answered. "I don't know, Rudi. I may have to promise them not to say anything. You'd better not count on it."

Rudi flushed briefly beneath his shining skin. "Promise?" he rasped. "Don't be sil-ly, Sand. What is a promise when you are dealing with people like that? You weren't above taking

their money on the black market, were you, a few years ago?"
He eyed Sand triumphantly. "No, there is no time these days
for sil-ly principles." He slapped his chamois gloves upon the
table, his distempered face in that instant an emblem of the
infectious selfishness eating at all Europe from within.

"I don't know," Sand repeated, condemning the other in
his heart, yet half believing him. He gazed at Rudi, certain
now that the man would refuse to help him; but to his surprise
he perceived that Rudi was still interested and was, in all prob-
ability, already possessed of still another solution beneficial to
himself, for there now appeared on his soft continental face a
vague tracery of amusement.

"Well," Rudi said, "I see there will be nothing for me in
this stupid business, but I am a gentleman, and I will keep my
word." He rose abruptly from the table. "It may take a little
time," he added, "to arrange things. I can reach you at home?"
He glanced at a gold watch, displayed gold cuff links. "Don't
be impatient," he said. "You will hear from me."

He smiled and departed, and another man followed him
out of the bar.

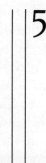

5

Two days later Sand received a letter from his father. It concerned Sand's failure, some months before in America, to obtain a position with a government agency.

Shortly after filing his application Sand had been called to the Capitol and interviewed. The interviewer was an inauspicious man in a side office who endeavored to fix Sand with a steely eye. He understood, he said, that Sand was an acquaintance of a man named Jacobi, and he wanted to know just what the relationship had been, putting his questions in a way that suggested anticipatory disbelief. Sand pointed out that his age at the time had been fourteen, but the interviewer seemed less concerned with this information than with the handsome watch on his own wrist, and his sole response was a meaningful suck of air through his front teeth. A few weeks later Sand received a tactful letter informing him that the job had been eliminated as an economy measure, and thanking him for his interest. He was dismayed to realize that his own country found him untrustworthy, and especially on such specious grounds.

Sand, though he shared the surface skepticism of his generation, felt the most sincere loyalty toward his country and a respect akin to reverence for the old, bright pages of its history. Therefore his rejection by his own nation was much more than a surprise or a disappointment, and confused him.

Subsequently, through the father of a friend, he had obtained the position with the wire service and was sent to Paris.

Meanwhile his father had looked into the affair, and by his own account of the meeting with Jacobi, unsolicited by his son, had dismissed official doubts and set up the possibility of an interesting post for Sand in his own branch of the foreign service. It was apparent, however, that Mr. Sand retained a few doubts of his own, for he wrote, in part,

> You understand, of course, that if you decide to accept this post you must immediately forswear all loyalties not in accord with our national interest. Doubtless you have long since done so, since you were prepared to enter government service some months ago. Nevertheless I feel it my duty to talk with you before you apply a second time. I would not be honest with myself or with our country if I did not take into account the impression made upon you by Jacobi, or honest with you if I claimed to believe, in view of your subsequent political uncertainty, that that impression had entirely worn away.

These lines, black and bold under the letterhead of the nation, were inscribed between wide white margins, as if his father, now an Under-Secretary of State, was preparing his correspondence for posterity—and as if, beneath that noble emblem, one could write safely only in the ornate, not-quite-candid manner of the statesman. The context itself was irritating, the more so because Sand knew, and knew his father knew, that he had not forsworn a thing, nor felt it necessary in terms of his integrity to do so.

He remembered how, five years before, in 1948, his father had startled Sand by initiating a discussion of Jacobi that he must have known would undermine his case against the man. And he had done this, Sand reflected, with a stubborn, stoic honesty born of the same idealism that led him now, responsible to the nation for his son, to be dishonest. Or so it seemed to Sand, who knew his father would not concede the paradox. In both instances Mr. Sand could claim, quite rightly, to have done what he thought best.

At that time Jacobi had recently left America.

"I saw him at the boat," Mr. Sand had said, interrupting a contemplation of their dinner. His son had known immediately to whom he referred, and, waiting, returned his brandy, untouched, to the table. He guessed as well that whatever the other had in mind was the purpose of their meeting. Sand had returned from Prague the previous day to find the invitation from his father, then in Paris on a mission. They had cocktails at the Crillon Bar and dinner at Laperouse.

"He sent you his regards, Edwin," said Mr. Sand, observing his son through the smoke of his cigar.

"Jacobi?"

"Yes. On that particular day I happened to be aboard his ship, seeing somebody off—the French emissary, I believe."

"Oh. And you ran into him."

"No, as a matter of fact, I looked him up. I felt I owed him something for his help to you that day in Perpignan."

Sand's face made no secret of his surprise.

"Is that so astonishing, Edwin?"

"I'm not sure. I thought you—" He stopped when his father smiled. "How was he?" he said finally.

"Rather upset. He had just given that speech of his about not believing in 'my country, right or wrong' to the reporters. When I turned up, he was in the process of showing them out."

Sand smiled himself. "And you, of course, he was very pleased to see," he said.

Mr. Sand extinguished his cigar, squashing it with an expression of distaste into the ashtray. Then he sat forward and said quietly, "Yes, in a way, I think he was. He was very much alone, you see. I'll be damned if I didn't feel sorry for the fellow. At any rate, I told him I considered myself still in his debt, and I asked if there wasn't some service I might do him."

"Did he know what you were talking about?"

"No, he didn't. He said that not only was I talking non-sense—he chose a more violent expression—but that I must consider him very stupid. You see, Edwin, he imagined I was making some sort of overture from the government, in case he might have considered defection from the Party."

"Were you?"

"Not at all. I really felt I owed him something. Or, rather, I didn't *want* to feel I owed him anything any longer, if you see what I mean—so that I could attack him in front of *you* without bad conscience."

"But you often have!"

"Precisely."

"But there's no reason why you shouldn't!" Sand exclaimed.

"Perhaps not. But I'm old-fashioned, I suppose." Mr. Sand made a deprecating gesture with his hand. "That's all rubbish, it doesn't matter, Edwin. But, as I was saying, I honestly believe the man was glad I came."

"I'd never guess it, from your description. Does he still call you 'Your Excellency'?"

"No. In fact, he became abusive—extremely abusive. I felt obliged to leave. But, believe it or not, he followed me to the gangplank and called out to me as I descended. When I came back, he became quite red in the face, and I thought he meant to assault me. But he only said, 'Please give my regards to Barney.'

" 'Barney?' I said. 'I'm not sure I know whom you mean.' "
Here Mr. Sand paused to light a fresh cigar, and smiled. His
humor, once so sharp-tongued and destructive, had been
gentled by the years. Though mannered still, it had a reflective, rueful tone better suited to the changes in the man, whom
Sand had seen chastened by each advancement, each increase
in responsibility for the uncertain future.

"I'm commonly known as Barney," Sand remarked.

"So he informed me," said his father.

Sand laughed obligingly. "And that was all?"

"Well, I thought so, but just as I was preparing to depart
a second time the fellow whispered, 'Listen, if you're sincere,
thanks very much. But there isn't much to be done.' He was
whispering, I am certain, because there was somebody close
by attempting to overhear him."

"But how did he mean that?"

"I don't know. The remark left me somewhat at a loss, and
so I took his hand and wished him good luck—and do you
know, Edwin, I believe I meant it sincerely at the time. That
man is forceful, no question about it. It is difficult not to respect him, at least—even as an enemy."

"I know," Sand said, returning his father's intent, unsmil-
ing gaze.

"At which point," Mr. Sand resumed, raising his voice a
little, "Jacobi said, 'I'm going to miss my country,' in a very
curious tone, as if he wanted at least one countryman, even
myself, to know this. And then he was gone." When his son
made no comment but stared straight ahead, reflecting, Mr.
Sand continued, "I only mention that last remark because it
isn't as obvious as it seems. Jacobi is a ruthless man, Edwin,
and he was close to tears. And on the strength of this incident,
I looked in on those espionage hearings a few weeks later."

"You mean he was accused of espionage?"

"Don't you read the papers? No, actually he wasn't accused, though he may as well have been. The ex-member of the Party on the witness stand was content to implicate him." Mr. Sand massaged an eye with a middle finger. "It seems that this repentant individual knew nothing of espionage himself, and having become, as he took the trouble to point out, an honest, God-fearing American, his sensitive conscience would not permit him to swear *with absolute certainty* that Jacobi had betrayed his country. The newspapers, of course, were far less delicate."

"Well, did he have anything at all on Jacobi?"

"He said simply that Jacobi was approached by an espionage agent after his return from Spain—or, rather, from France—in 1938. The conversation was apparently unpleasant and quite brief, and was passed along the Party grapevine, and memorized by our God-fearing witness, whose recollection in such matters was well-nigh uncanny. He paraphrased it something like this—

" 'Espionage?' Jacobi said.

" 'We don't call it that.'

" 'I'll have to think it over.'

" 'Are you afraid, or do you disapprove of it?'

" 'Do you think I'm afraid?'

" 'That would be better. Otherwise I must infer that you oppose the Party's will.'

" 'I don't have to prove my allegiance to the Party, not after sixteen years. I'll think it over.'

" 'After sixteen years you should know better what allegiance to the Party means. You will please forget this conversation.'

"But apparently," Mr. Sand resumed, "according, once again, to our trusty witness, Jacobi returned the following day to see this agent. It's not known what took place. Which brings me to a final, interesting point neglected by the newspapers: the witness also testified that, dating from this interview, Jacobi was under suspicion, though apparently unaware of it himself, and that, dating from Jacobi's departure for Europe, that suspicion became official policy. He was referred to in slighting terms by the leaders, and his various exploits in Spain and in World War Two were belittled, even though, at this very moment, the Party journal was defending him and decrying his departure! Which would seem to me conclusive proof that he never joined the underground, whether he wanted to or not."

"Obviously he didn't want to," Sand said. "But I'm surprised that he hesitated. He didn't strike me as the man to object to method." He was thinking at that moment of Jacobi's pronouncements in Perpignan, and shook his head, bewildered. He felt tired and depressed, a condition he attributed to the brandy.

"That's it, you see," his father said. "That's what makes him such an enigma. Remember his remark to me at the boat, Edwin." Mr. Sand paused a moment, inspecting his cigar. "I'm tempted to believe that, however mistaken, that man is a patriot, not of the vocal variety so prevalent today, but in the true sense—that is, he is willing to sacrifice himself to what he considers to be the national interest. For all we know, he might be a sort of twentieth-century John Brown. But like John Brown," Mr. Sand concluded pointedly, "he is in the wrong, and history will judge him accordingly."

At that time, having just come from Czechoslovakia, Barney Sand was inclined to agree. Yet it seemed to him possible, on the one hand, that Jacobi knew little of the methods of the Party as practiced once it was in power, and might well consider such methods a betrayal of Party doctrine. He preferred to think so. And, on the other hand, he suspected that his father had now made his essential point, and that the fairness with which he had treated Jacobi stemmed in part from the realization that Jacobi's influence on his son could only be dispelled once the enemy was given his due. Therefore Sand, instead of nodding, shrugged his shoulders and said nothing.

They sat a little while in silence.

"However," Mr. Sand resumed at last, "I very much dislike the whole business if, as I suspect, Jacobi is being pilloried on both sides for doing what he thought right. Because you see, Edwin, that as a result of the incident with the underground he finds himself rejected not only by his country—and I believe that this pains him terribly, though he must have known he was running that risk—but by his comrades. Of course, he is probably still unaware of the second loss."

"You think the Party will expel him, then?"

"Sooner or later. Yes, I do."

Mr. Sand sat back in his chair and signaled to the waiter. He received the check, glanced at it, and reached for his billfold with impatience, as if the waiter were cheating him of time required to anayze his son's expression.

"There is no doubt, in my mind at least," the letter of five years later read, "that I came out unfavorably in the comparison Jacobi forced upon you then. The point is, in short, that I cannot in good conscience recommend you to the foreign service until I am certain of your allegiance—not to myself as opposed to Jacobi, for that is your affair, but to the concept of the national interest which I represent. I pray to God that your choice will be the right one."

Here was his father's official side, with the self-consciousness of its ideals, its reduction of political integrity to protocol, as if no man could determine his ethics for himself, but must choose between black and white.

This man whose Spartan honesty conceded his son's allegiance to the enemy, and even the enemy's sincerity, could call out simultaneously for loyalty to himself and to his narrow code, and, enmeshed in his own eloquence, solicit the aid of God in doing so. The latter recourse seemed to Sand especially annoying.

Nevertheless, he respected his father—that private individual, at least, too honest to flesh out the bone of ethics with compromise, compromise with hypocrisy, and hypocrisy with the rotten fat of righteousness. For even in this letter, the bone bit through that fat like a hard white tooth protruding from soft gum.

And because he respected him, Sand was all the more disturbed by the implication that he himself might fail his country. Certainly this was not the case. He had only to glance at American history, hear the names of its rivers and towns, feel and smell its winds and weather, to know an exultation, and though much of his life had been passed abroad, he thought of America as home and never questioned that he would return there one day for good, to work for the government, perhaps, and to marry and raise a family.

Such doubts as he had were concerned not with politics and nations, but with society. If, as Jacobi claimed, most human beings were allowed to live like dogs, if responsibility ran far behind the people's need, then the world fed its own unrest, like fever, and that fever could not be obscured, or cured, by politics.

It seemed to Sand that as long as he kept this point in fair perspective he might hope to see things clearly in his world. But perspective was prey to expedience, like truth. One needed conscience as well as courage, and his conscience, he felt, was no longer the strong quantity that it had been when he had known Jacobi. At that age, with no need to be practical, one could look at things directly. But later one was driven toward retreat, toward expedience hawked like fool's gold by one's elders, who, themselves defeated, could no longer look idealism in the eye. And their cynicism, mistaken often for maturity, served to conceal awareness of forsaken codes which, however impractical, they knew in their hearts to be still valid.

Sand himself, at twenty-nine, was idealistic still, but increasingly conscious of losing ground. Over the years he had grown less angry at injustice, more ready to accept what his editor, two days before, had termed "the facts of life." Traveling back and forth across the world, a student, a soldier, a student once again, and now in the third of three lackluster jobs, his rough edges had been rounded off, his vision scuffed and scarred. He knew this and resented his own frailty. Today the incidents that had shocked him in the past seemed trivial and faraway—were they exaggerated then, or was he equivocating now?

Impressions of childhood, revolving around the servants— the ones he thought were too old to have to work, who sent the family Christmas cards long after they had gone and been forgotten, who called him "Mr. Edwin" even when, a senseless child, he insulted them or hurt their feelings, who answered to names like Margaret and Marie, answered as promptly, faithfully, as the family spaniel, although considered to have less personality, and not nearly so beloved.

At school and at college and in the army he pursued his education in the niceties of cruelty and selfishness. As a young man in advertising, between 1949 and 1951, he had changed positions twice because he did not like the work enough to curb his tongue, and, feeling purified, had set free a fiancée for the same reason.

In his uneventful life Sand had become angry, spoken out, been mollified on a number of occasions. But he felt now that he had spoken out too seldom and too safely and been resigned too readily. Yet among the incidents that involved him personally only one still kept something of its first effect upon him, for the injustice here had seemed a part of his inheritance, a caul, and had bewildered him.

It occurred near the summer resort that he later described to Jacobi. There was a home there for spastic children, on a wide lawn beside a marshy pond, and he had passed it often on his bicycle, unaware of what it was.

One August morning, pedaling down the road, he heard a high, harsh crying, and saw, in the middle of the pond, a boy crouched in a rowboat. There was a single oar floating near the boat, and though the boy held the other he made no effort to retrieve its mate, but gesticulated furiously, crying out.

Barney walked down to the edge of the pond and shouted at the boy to paddle toward the other oar. But the boy only cried out even louder, in strange unintelligible sounds that made no sense to Barney at all. It came to him then that the boy was a spastic, and, though he had no very clear idea of what a spastic might be, he realized the other's helplessness with a start of fear. When the boy cried out again, Barney made his way out across the marshy edges of the pond.

It was a very hot, humid day, and from beneath his sunken tennis shoes there rose to his nostrils the thick, viscous stench of the rotten bog. The muck sucked heavily at his legs, and once he fell forward on his hands. In his panic and increasing fear he imagined himself sinking forever into this stew of corrupt earth, and struggled forward on hands and knees toward the muddy water. There he swam painfully toward the rowboat, touching from time to time sunken hummocks of unknown matter and clinging grasses and once, he was positive, a live loathsome creature of considerable size. He reached the boat in a frenzy of speed and hauled himself, gasping, over the side.

The boy in the boat was crouched in the stern, his twisted face alight with any number of emotions, each striving to dominate his expression. Barney, afraid and fascinated, watched the passage of fear and hysteria and gratitude and shame and, worst of all, the terrible desire to be accepted as another boy and not as a human outcast. But in his efforts toward this end, the boy only compromised his position, for he emitted a series of excited yelps that scared Barney out of his wits, and only momentarily calmed down enough to push out a squeaky "Thank you." Then he was off again, his legs thrashing crazily in the bilge water, employing every inch of his person to convey to Barney his message, until the latter managed a nod and a smile, and, still shaken, paddled the rowboat to the drifting oar.

As Barney rowed back across the pond, the boy in the stern was silent, staring at him with such infinite sadness and a kind of hopeless love that Barney would almost have preferred the preceding experience. He maintained his friendly smile, however, and managed to speak for the first time, saying in a choked voice, "It wasn't your fault, losing the oar like that, it could happen to anybody. And I got a swim out of it too, so we're even." The boy clearly understood him, and understood, too, Barney's sympathy, for he burst into tears and a moment later tried once again to speak. But once again coordination failed him, and he repeated the mistake of trying to convey with body and soul what was already clear in his expression. In the process he very nearly fell into the water, but, oblivious, continued to cry out in his heartbreaking way until, exhausted, he became subdued again and clutched the gunwales in silence until they reached the dock.

There a man was waiting for them. He thanked Barney for himself and the boy, and explained that this boy was his best patient, could maneuver a rowboat, and even speak coherently as long as he didn't try too hard or become excited. The man spoke in front of the boy, and doubtless in part for his benefit, but the latter smiled in any case, glancing shyly at

Barney as if in new hope of friendship. They watched each other one long painful moment. Then Barney took the boy's hand in his own and shook it, ashamed of an inward wincing away from the touch of the cripple's flesh. He moved away, heart pounding, across the silent lawn, conscious of a breathless censure in the institution's yellow face, and up the steep side of the ditch to the public road, fleeing this unknown world of human misery, regaining the rich guilty realm of sunlight and peaceful summer.

He couldn't get over the idea that the spastic was a boy of his own age, and apparently intelligent. How alike they were in all valid respects, yet how far apart in that slight, unjust difference between them! The loss of the oar was only a token of innumerable deeper losses. And there they had stood, staring at each other across a void, and when Barney had reached out to the other, had taken his hand, the touch had been not an affirmation of kinship with a fellow creature but, rather, a morbid gesture, compulsive and disagreeable.

He had even, unwillingly, despised the other's clothes. Barney was dressed like all the sunburned boys he knew, in khaki shorts, white polo shirt, white socks and sneakers. By contrast this stranger had been arrayed in a grotesque gaiety of colors. Above bright yellow swimming trunks he wore a shirt striped orange and green, and the gleaming shorts pinched tight on a pair of sick white legs, which disappeared in turn into blue socks and high black hard-soled shoes. This difference in their costumes had created in Barney's mind a distinction between them that confused and shamed him and drove him to jar his bicycle into pits at the side of the road. He swore to himself that he would visit the boy again and share with him his now oppressive health, and wealth, if possible. But of course he did not return. The failure was a normal one, but Barney felt guilty for the rest of that summer and later. He thought often of the boy as a sort of secret self—the cries, the thrashing that might still be going on, the need of assistance and friendship—and that desperate face became for him a touchstone of human misery and defeat.

The sense of the struggle around him was focused by Jacobi's words of two years later, and dramatized by his prediction of revolt. Sand recalled the flight north from Barcelona, the blaring horn of the big limousine cutting its swift swath through the peasant caravans, and the hot black Iberian eyes beneath the black berets and shawls, which stared, submissive still, as they passed through—the people, Jacobi's people, their long patience close to its end.

Sand had long since been convinced that the Party was in the wrong, but because of Jacobi's sincere allegiance to it he feared that his own mind might be a product of the times, that, despite his trip to Prague, he had not come honestly by his conclusion, and that once again he had been brought around too readily by majority opinion. And he feared as well that he might now be faced with his final chance to prove his integrity to himself by putting it to a test.

He was determined, therefore, to see Jacobi before repudiating the man's cause. He knew in his heart that his resolve might not last, that his time was short. Even now timidity insinuated itself, half persuading him of his editor's convictions—that his project was halfwitted, dangerous, doomed to failure. But his uneasiness only made him angry and more stubborn about the search.

In response to his father's letter, he wrote his decision to remain in his present job, at least for the time being. By this time he had done what he had long since intended to do—he had purchased and read the basic Party texts, and sentenced himself to wander on the barrens, bleak and lonely, of reflection.

For the remainder of the week Sand walked a good deal and thought too much, picking at his misgivings and plucking his courage from the reach of dread. He traveled the ordered areas not too distant from his building, absorbing from the fall quiet of the Tuileries, the nineteenth-century stateliness of the Parc Monçeau, the muted age of the Palais Royal, a certain harmony, which tempted him to believe that the state of the world he had always known was only a passing squall of history and not, as Jacobi proclaimed, the first skirmishes of the Great Twentieth-Century War.

But late one afternoon, after leaving the Louvre, he walked out on the Pont du Carrousel. There something happened which, though unimportant, disturbed him more than he let himself admit.

Two swift black birds had cut the twilight sinking to the river and swept in his direction. The second, a falcon, soared before stooping on the other. It struck almost delicately, veered upward and away, and did not circle, as if hastening to regain some far migration route toward the south. But the pigeon fell broken-backed into the Seine. It fluttered a moment near the bank before disappearing with the current beneath the bridge.

Sand, startled, stepped across the bridge, to confirm the death in the appearance of the floating bird on the other side. But the pigeon never came, and he found himself descending the stone steps to the quai. Turning, he saw in the shadows beneath the arch a figure kneeling at the water's edge, silhouetted against the river. The figure, glimpsing him, clutched the pigeon to its breast and scurried back into the darkness by the wall.

Night was coming on, and he went home.

The acquisitive face of Rudi Gleize, appearing that evening at his door, completed his misgivings.

"Pack a small suitcase," Rudi said, "and lock your door. You will not be back for a little while."

Rudi slipped back onto the landing and listened until Sand was ready, then led him down in silence into the dark.

6

They crossed the river at the Pont du Carrousel and entered the broken maze of antique Paris by the rue des Saints-Pères. Soon they turned left and were making their way east, paralleling the quais. They passed on their right the miniature Place Furstemberg and again turned left. It seemed to Sand that they were circling on their tracks, and he could not determine whether Rudi was unfamiliar with the area or whether he was purposely trying to confuse him in this ancient quarter. The route they were now traveling was no more than an alley, knifing high and narrow into the black September sky, but soon it came out on a wider street. They crossed, continuing through a side way flanked by littered picture galleries and halting at last at the angle of two more streets. Down the dark stretches of one he made out the quai, the headlights of occasional cars shaping up its walls, two bookstalls, a small plane tree, and the late walkers. Rudi Gleize took out a cigarette and lit it, and the flame of the match revealed a nervous winking of his eyes.

"Why won't you tell me where we're going?" Sand demanded, for the second time.

"We're here," Rudi said making a vague gesture toward the walls of the corner building.

"You mean Jacobi is being kept right here?"

"Don't be sil-ly," Rudi said. His nervousness and resultant irritation led him to give himself away, for then he muttered, "Do you think if I knew where Jacobi was I'd bother myself with all this stupid running around?" He said it almost to himself, glancing about him in all directions and catching his breath at the far sound of footfalls around the corner.

Sand noticed that from their vantage point they could observe four different approaches, and knew now why Rudi had stopped and why they had walked here. But the streets were empty, and after a moment Rudi moved rapidly away along the wall and disappeared into the first entrance on the street leading down to the quai. Sand, following, glanced back at the marker on the corner: RUE DES GRANDS AUGUSTINS.

Rudi awaited him by the stairwell. "These are friends of mine, a sculptor and his wife," he whispered. "You will live with them while this business continues. Do not tell them any more than you have to, and do not get in touch with your news agency or anybody else." His conspiratorial tone was annoying to Sand, and yet Sand knew that he himself was too relaxed, too unprepared, and tried to key himself up to the significance of his mission. He was nervous, yes, but more at the thought of meeting strangers than of entering upon the hunt.

And the people who greeted them on the fourth landing were immediately so sympathetic to him, so warm and charming, that Rudi's posturings seemed more nonsensical than ever.

"This is Lise," Rudi whispered, "and this is Olivier." Sand was not told their surnames. For the moment he tried to guess their attitude toward Rudi Gleize and their position in respect to him, hoping thereby to sharpen his own insight into the validity of Rudi's methods.

Olivier was a thin dark man whose natural expression of kindly grief might have done credit to a clown. A shambling torpid manner was offset by bright, bushy-browed eyes, which regarded Rudi Gleize with mixed caution and contempt. There was no contempt, however, in the face of the woman called Lise. She sat Rudi down with every evidence of respect and affection, but in such an exaggerated manner that Sand suspected, unwillingly, that these people were in Rudi's pay.

"Ah, dear Rudi," she said, "it's been so long since you have come to us, but at least you have brought us the company of your friend!"

Olivier observed her, hands in pockets, his sad mouth twitching in amusement, and exchanged a compassionate glance with Sand when she turned upon the latter and, seizing him warmly by the shoulders, forced him back into a second chair, from which, foresightedly, the sculptor had dumped two sleeping cats. Sand guessed immediately that, despite Rudi's precaution, this pair had a very good idea of the project at hand, for Olivier smiled again, just visibly, when at the conclusion of a long, roundabout conversation directed by Rudi Gleize it was agreed by all, for no good reason, that Sand should move in immediately as a lodger. The decision was celebrated with a bottle of red wine, which Rudi scarcely touched. He sat drumming his fingers upon the table, and acted out his part as a sociable companion with the sole aid of a fixed, unhealthy grin.

Sand took careful note of his surroundings. The room was the heart of the apartment, for the dinner remains and reading matter and bits of clothing all had an air of permanence on the huge black table that almost filled the room. There was a makeshift kitchen squashed against one wall, a charcoal stove, a soft, defeated armchair barely visible beneath a heap of books and sketches, art journals, shoes, and bits of string, and a cabinet manned by three large cats, an orange, a gray, and a Persian. Shoulder to shoulder, inflaming the walls, were posters, calendars, and paintings, inscribed in vivid strokes to the woman Lise, now drinking wine in expansive fashion at the end of the table. And in the corner, suspicious in its freshness, was a made-up cot.

Lise was a full-haunched, graceful woman in her late thirties who might once have been an entertainer. She had a theatrical gusto and a low, attractive voice and an air of fresh discovery of pleasure that could not quite offset her betrayal by flesh and drink. Yet Sand found himself strongly attracted to her. Her face, he thought, though compromised by the fact that no especial care was taken of it, remained quite beautiful. The figure she cut was ample and baroque, and a subtle licentiousness in her manner hinted at more than he felt he ought to know.

Sand watched her until she smiled at him. Averting his gaze, he caught the eye of Olivier, neither cynical nor reproving, but understanding.

Sand had seen Rudi to the door.

"She knew Jacobi," Rudi told him, "and she knows another man, a Party leader, who may decide to help you. Do not be hasty, my dear Sand, and do not take any action on your own, for my sake."

"For your sake, Rudi?"

"Of course." Rudi smiled despite himself. "I feel responsible for you, you understand?"

"Not yet, I must admit. There is something you are not telling me."

"Don't be sil-ly," Rudi said. "What is there for me in this crazy business?" He nodded, smiling again, and went away down the stairs.

"Will I see you again?" Sand called, uneasy.

But Rudi did not answer.

Olivier and Lise were still seated at the table when he

returned. "You have known our Rudi for some time?" Lise inquired. Her tone was ambiguous, and Olivier frowned, then laughed aloud.

"Yes, for several years." Sand paused. "It must be very inconvenient for you, my staying here, madame."

"I assure you it is not, dear friend!" Startled, a little frightened even, she rose from her chair and filled his glass with wine. "A *gros rouge*," she said, "will make you feel right at home."

"Yes, we are delighted," Olivier said quietly. "Not only because"—he made an uncertain gesture with his hand—"we are so indebted to Monsieur Gleize, but because we are glad of your company." He said this graciously, without affectation, and, Sand could not help feeling, with some sincerity.

"*Rudi*," Lise corrected him.

"*Ru-di*," Olivier repeated slowly, with expressionless distaste, as if he were holding the word at arm's length, dangled from his fingertips like a dead mouse. The opinion was conveyed so economically that Sand could not help but smile, and was pleased when Olivier returned the smile and Lise winked at him. They did not mention Rudi Gleize again.

The red wine in the third bottle fell away to nothing, and with it their conversation. The gray cat sprang silently from the top of the cabinet and landed on the table between them with an ominous thump, stretched itself, mouth wide, and sat, tail twitching, watching Sand.

"He wants your chair," Lise said, and yawned herself.

"We should go to bed, I suppose," Sand said, and Olivier nodded. When Lise had gone, parting a curtain into another room, Olivier led Sand to the bathroom and showed him in passing his own studio. "A great deal of good material has gone into that room," he remarked. "It's a pity that nothing worth while has ever come out of it." He smiled before Sand could answer.

Sand rose early the next morning and went out to get his breakfast. He went inland from the quai, up the rue Saint-André-des-Arts, and turned off into the rue de Buci. There, from his table in a small café, he could observe the Buci market place and the faces of his new neighborhood. These were very different from the Right Bank faces, less obsequious and much less disagreeable, and there were representatives of every class on this noisy common ground. He had a comfortable feeling of being one of them, and, after his coffee, strolled up and down among the stalls. From there he wandered down the rue de Seine and came out on the river opposite the Louvre.

Turning, he surveyed by daylight the maze into which Rudi had led him the evening before, but there was no sign of it. On his left loomed the massive Institut and down to his right the open garden of the Beaux Arts. He was once again in the public Paris, the impersonal Paris, and his new quarter, personal and unpredictable, lurked somewhere behind these façades. He moved up the quai and re-entered the quarter, with excitement and misgiving, by the river end of the rue des Grands Augustins.

Lise and Olivier were relieved to see him. Lise was sleepy and irritable, clutching the curtain to her bedroom for support. In the early morning her age had the upper hand in her expression, and her aging bathrobe was not up to the task of concealing her lowered bosom. Still, there was something sensual, naïvely provocative, in her stance, and Sand suffered once more a pang of cupidity, which his cheerful air could not hide from Olivier.

"*Il y reste encore quelque chose, ma petite.*" The latter smiled. "*Et moi, ton petit Olivier, c'est bien moi qui te salue!*" He spoke in the thick accent of Provence, gesturing heavily with his hands, and plunged into a breathless monologue. "Yes, yes, yes, it is I, your dear Olivier, who congratulates you, splendid Lise of the beautiful dawn!"

"Idiot! That's enough of your nonsense. You are a stupid good-for-nothing. It is only my promise to your old mother that keeps me here, but someday you will go too far!"

"No, no, no, it is clear you do not understand! It is I, your sweet little Olivier, who declares his passion!"

"Pig! It is clear that you have brought shame to me in the entire neighborhood, and ill health besides! And I didn't have to sacrifice myself, as everybody knows; there were others lying at my feet!"

"Others, yes. Many others, it is true. Too many others for the good wives of the village, as was well known—and spending their sous for the honor too, it should be said! But there, I forgive your sins because I am your cherished, your precious little Olivier, and I am all you have in the world now that you are old and ugly."

"You are an imbecile and a drunken sot, and I wash my hands of you and your filthy old mother, who got my virgin's promise by trickery and false claims of your inheritance. But there are limits to my virtue, understand me well, and I know where to go to be appreciated!"

"To be sure you do, you have always known, and been well paid for it too, it should be said! Limits to your virtue, yes, indeed—but as to the virgin's promise, I do not understand you, your terms confuse me slightly, under the circumstances which the neighborhood, for one, knows better than I! But there, never mind, I will not forsake you now that you are stupid and fat and interested only in the bottle, for I am your superb, your generous-hearted little Olivier, and I am in the process of declaring my great love for you, if only you would have the wit to listen, for obviously you will not hear it from a man again."

Olivier stopped suddenly and gazed at Lise, who had been laughing quietly in the doorway. But she stopped laughing and, glancing at Sand, flushed impatiently. "You're impossi-

ble," she muttered at Olivier. "It's too early in the morning
for your nonsense." She disappeared behind the curtain, and
Olivier stared after her. He had clearly forgotten about Sand,
and turned, surprised, at the sound of the other's laughter.
This was Sand's first experience with Olivier's fantasies and
masquerades, and he could not have guessed their emotional
dimensions in the heart of the other man. Later he would see
the despair of Olivier the sculptor, which promoted these
flights into unreality and made a minor art of them.

Olivier was much more interesting than Lise, though he
seldom took part in normal conversation. He preferred to leap
up from the table and describe a pattern of intricate gyrations
around the room, his hands alive in neat, quick parodies of
operatic gestures lust, love, vulgar dramas, storms, fish, animals, people in the streets—all of life like clay in the deft
mime of his fingers, and his voice the while remarking ani-
matedly on endless unrelated subjects, singing, sighing, or
breaking off in sudden laughter as he left the room. In seconds
he would return again, his features transformed by masks, false
faces, eyebrows, wrinkles, and red noses, so cleverly applied
that he was never twice the same nor ever quite implausible.
He had a depthless repertoire of gaits and voices, gestures and
inflections, and an array of improbable garments, which covered the walls of the outer hallway and made of him a church-
man at one moment and a grandmother the next, according
to his whim. But he seemed to favor the outcasts of society,
the tramps and beggars, prostitutes and drunks, and went
through their futile motions with exalted finesse, without cruelty or sarcasm, forsaking caricature for humor, and executing
the whole with such pure grace that the spectator, laughing,
also felt moved to tears. And Olivier himself, quietly resuming
his seat, would sink at once into a gloom so remote that Sand
would not dare to talk to him, but converse with Lise on important topics that no longer seemed important.

Sand visited with Olivier the small galleries of the quarter and a number of cafés and antique shops. Olivier seemed loath to leave his immediate district, turning back when they approached the quais or Saint-Germain-des-Prés. They would pause for a moment at the end of the rue de l'Ancienne Comédie, gazing out upon the wide, bright boulevard like two observers from a more cloistered world, then turn back into the narrow, shadowed streets toward the Seine.

Olivier knew most of the people they passed, who seemed to regard him with great amusement and affection. Their reaction to his elaborate greetings reaffirmed Sand's own immediate liking for the man. And Sand himself felt close to the people here. He talked with a butcher who sang in cabarets, a flower-seller deformed by German torture who lectured on love at the Institut Géographique, the mad, forsaken wife of a voguish surrealist—but also with the art-dealers, antique-sellers, various old men, mystics, intellectuals, alcoholics, and with a number of dogs and children partial to Olivier. As time went on they accepted him without Olivier, calling out to him in the street, and once when, in a café, he was asked the time, and answered, exuberant in his wine, as he had been answered long ago, they roared and repeated aloud among themselves, "*Mais qu'est-ce que ça peut te faire, mon petit, puisque ça change tout le temps!*"

He hadn't thought of the remark as that amusing, though he laughed himself and bowed, somewhat guiltily, to their new opinion of him as a humorous American.

"*Mais comme il est drôle, cet américain!*"

He was forced to accept a cognac which he knew the donor could not afford, and, walking home, he imagined that he could live quite happily with Olivier and Lise forever.

But they talked of Jacobi that very evening. Lise slyly introduced the name into a general discussion of the Party, alert for Sand's reaction

"You know Jacobi, then?" Sand asked.

"Jacobi? Oh yes, quite well. I haven't seen him in some time—"

"So much the worse for you both," Olivier interrupted under his breath.

"That's enough, Olivier. No, not since the late thirties, really. He came out of Spain and stayed with us for a little while, in the Pays-Basque. Then I think he went back to America."

"He came back during the war, your Jacobi," Olivier said. "He worked with the Resistance, in the South. I saw him myself, near Carcassonne."

Lise stared at him. "Why didn't you tell me this?" she whispered.

Olivier said, "You ask a good deal of me, dear Lise." He relapsed into silence.

"What sort of man was he?" Sand asked, uncomfortable. He had intended a tactful change of subject, but a baleful glance from Olivier demonstrated to him that he had, instead, worsened the situation. Then Olivier rose abruptly and crossed the hallway to his studio.

Lise watched him go with an expression of regret, but clearly her mind was elsewhere. "Ah, ce Jacobi," she began, half to herself, "c'était un homme, vous savez, celui-là." She remained silent for a time, touching the fingers of her hands together, then placing them on her collarbones. The gesture, indicating as it did her proprietary interest in the soul of the man, was affected, almost theatrical. Sand was to notice that whenever Lise spoke of Jacobi she adopted a tone that made of their relation a profound and meaningful thing, not to be fathomed easily by outsiders, and very creditable to herself into the bargain. But her vanity was so childlike, so simple-hearted, that he found it touching rather than irritating, and liked her all the more because of it.

"We in this country have a very distinct notion of what a man must be," she was saying. "There are not so many of them, I assure you. Jacobi, and, in his way, my Olivier—I haven't known many others. Marat, perhaps, though I wonder sometimes if Marat can be counted."

Sand waited expectantly, and after a moment she said to him, "Marat is the man you are to meet. He is very important in the Party. We used to see a great deal of Marat." She shook her head. "He was a great friend of Jacobi."

"You and Olivier," Sand said, "you are with the Party, then?"

"No. We were. All we intellectuals were." Lise, who gave little sign of intellectuality, was very fond of this term. "But the Party has changed, you know, it is purely political now. It is like a young idealistic boy who has learned to compromise, to put ambition above the ideal."

Sand nodded at this obvious remark somewhat impatiently. "And Jacobi," he said, "has he changed too?"

"I don't know. I haven't seen him since before the war. But I don't think he could change, a man like that; he is too strong, and blinded by his strength. To tell you the truth, Jacobi is intelligent in a very narrow way. He sees only the people and their poverty, and to advance their hopes he will destroy everything, himself included. It is not the Party that is important to him, not really; he is not like Marat that way, not political. He has always followed his own path, Jacobi, and his ideals are old-fashioned now, and a little sad."

"I met him once, you know," Sand said. "I liked him very much."

"I loved him," Lise said quite simply. "Yes, though I knew it too late. But he was always solitary, his mind was elsewhere even when—" She flushed. "Yes, even then," she blurted angrily, as if admitting something to herself for the first time. "I couldn't forgive that in another man, and I've never had to."

She smiled reflectively, but her eyes were sad. "And, believe me, I have no complaints." She nodded her head in the direction of Olivier's studio. "Do not be misled by his childish manner. He is wise, and hopelessly merciful, my Olivier, and as great a man in his way as my Jacobi." Moved by her own eloquence, she coughed and took refuge in her wine.

7

In the course of that week Sand was sent to
a party. He did not know who was giving the party, and neither did Lise, who gave him the address and directions. Neither did he know what was expected of him, nor what his
approach should be. He could hardly go about asking, "Where
is Jacobi?"—and yet this was the information he had to have.
Of course he could ask leading questions, but, if for no other
reason than lack of experience, his powers of persiflage were
nil, and he knew it. They would see through him in a moment.
And he could not understand why Rudi—for certainly Rudi
was behind this—had not given him some guidance. Perhaps
Rudi would be there, although his instinct denied the possibility. Who, then? This man Marat? It did not seem likely
somehow. Uneasy, Sand passed down alien streets, cursing
Rudi and his mysteries and the whole impossible plan.

On the stairway he paused, struggling to control a sliding
feeling in his stomach. The building was scrofulous and dank,
and situated somewhere—he was not sure where—in the cob-
bled area beyond the Panthéon. He had somehow lost his
bearings. Sand knew nothing of this quarter, even by hearsay.
It had no characteristic stamp, as did other parts of Paris, of
students, bourgeois, foreign groups, demimonde, or even petty

commerce, but was amorphous, old and dark, a catchall and a melting pot. The voices he heard were the voices of many tongues, and the odors invidious and untraceable.

He moved upward again, hearing people below in the foyer. On the top floor a girl awaited him, laughing at nothing in the way certain hostesses have, from which Sand assumed mistakenly that she was drunk.

"English or American?" she cried. "Go ahead in." He realized that the girl did not know who he was, nor care. He took her hand self-consciously, but she was already laughing over his shoulder at the people behind him, a seedy blond girl in dungarees and sandals escorted by a young black man. The black grinned with the arrogance of terror.

"Well, Inga, my God, where did you find him! He's mar-velous!" When the hostess took both hands within her own, the two men exchanged a look of pain and suspicion. She was crooning, "Oh my God, but you're so mar-velous and black, how I'd love to have you for myself!" She shook her head, eyes squinted. "So lean and repellent and marvelous," she whispered, still clutching his hands, while the Swedish girl smiled in idiotic approval.

Entering, the black man said to Sand, "American?"

Sand nodded.

"Yeah," the other said, his gaze dancing nervously around the room, "yeah, me too." He took from his pocket a small metal box, from which he removed with great care a very thin handmade cigarette. Sand was on the point of offering one of his own when it occurred to him that there might be more to this disreputable item than met the eye. He watched the other light it and, pinching it between thumb and index finger, sip at it hastily several times before turning it over to the Swedish girl. She repeated the performance and returned it immediately to her companion, who offered it politely to Sand.

"What is it?" Sand said.

"Tea," the black said, surprised. "What you think I was gonna give you, man?"

"Hash-ish," the Swedish girl explained, reaching for it, but her companion withheld it from her, sucking at it furiously himself. "Cool," he whispered. He returned it to her grudgingly.

"Cool," the girl repeated. "Crazy, man." She spoke with a heavy accent that made the words even more grotesque and meaningless. And Sand, looking around, perceived that a number of people were smoking the "tea," and noticed the odor he had thought was incense, rich and delicate at once, a burning of exquisite leaves.

He managed to find himself a drink and then another, and, leaning against the wall, searched the cluttered room for some clue to his presence. But nobody approached him, and finally he moved out through the haze in hopes of becoming entangled in a conversation, for people had begun to notice him standing all alone. But the conversations he crossed were mindless, or unintelligible, or in some unfamiliar language. The room was heavy with the sweet reek of narcotics, and in a corner, openly and unnoticed by the others, a man was making love to a young girl already half undressed. The laughter in the place was out of control, a sort of high, fast *snee-snee-snee* but the voices were dulled and painfully slow, like gruntings from some prehistoric cave.

The grinning masks did not return his gaze but saw right past him as if he were invisible, and he suffered a swift annoyance veined with panic.

Sand sought out the black again, and, shaking him by the shoulder to get his attention, asked to try one of the cigarettes.

"Gone, man," the man muttered, "and takin' me right with him." It took him minutes to extract his box.

Nothing happened to Sand at first, and after a time he

forgot about the cigarette. He took another almost idly, pleased
to be relaxed at last, and talking. He was having a very good
time, and listened to his own voice laughing as if from a near
distance. After a time he forgot what he was talking about and
who he might be talking to, so delighted was he with a pattern
he had discovered in the rug. It was a beautiful pattern, rather
wistful and sad, but full of important meanings, and he was in
the process of interpreting it aloud, and being extraordinarily
humorous about it, when he discovered that he was standing
once again all by himself. The discovery tickled him afresh,
and he burst out in a shout of laughter and seated himself
upon the most meaningful part of the rug pattern to teach it
a lesson.

Then he felt a hand upon his arm and drifted obediently
to his feet and allowed himself to be led into another room
and sat upon a bed. There was a girl with him, quite a pretty
girl, and he saw in her eyes a sort of love he had never known
before, and which brought tears to his eyes. He was overcome
by her devotion to him, and repaid her by attempting to relate
a funny story. Then his face was slapped, and he heard a voice
breathing, "Leave me go, Sand, get hold of yourself, please,
now—" And he opened his eyes, no longer laughing, and
looked into the face of Sara Gleize.

"Feeling better?" she said to him. He wondered if he had
fallen asleep. He felt heavy in body and mind, and deeply
depressed. There was a movement behind him on the bed,
and he became aware of another couple, pressed together
against the wall, asleep. The girl was almost naked.

"You are not accustomed," Sara Gleize said to him in English. "You have too much. When I bring you in here, you
want to take my clothes." She giggled. Sand, awake and sober
behind his half-shut eyes, had the sense to keep silent until
he retrieved his bearings. He saw that Sara Gleize had a glass

in her hand and was very drunk. Sitting there on the edge of the double bed, she swayed precariously and several times was forced to brace herself, hand on Sand's chest.

"No good, tea parties," she was saying. "The beginning is all right, but last time I have that depression after, and try to kill myself." She spoke matter-of-factly, with clinical interest. "Here was a big Polish boy last week who kill himself. He has a big Dalmatian dog, and only for that dog, nobody know anything. He lock the door first, see, and everybody think he goes on a trip, but the dog smell him dead in there, and scratch at the door maybe three or four days before the concierge look in . . ." Her voice drifted away, returned. "He was a very nice boy, I like him too. And there are many here who do the same thing any moment. They don't know what they are doing in their life, these people; they are afraid and lost. In Prague also we had them. Everywhere in Europe they are, all hiding together like this in little holes. They think they are really living, only they are really dying. Like me."

She shook her head, losing her balance once again and sprawling on top of Sand. He put his arm around her, and she whispered in his ear, "Not now, Sand. We go to my place."

"How long have you spoken English, Sara?"

"You like it?" She giggled, then frowned. "No, I practice it only, to learn, you do not mind? It is American I speak. Everybody learn to speak American, because Americans have all the money. The cosh." She giggled again.

"*Cash*," he said. "What are you here for, Sara?"

"I keep my eye on you." She giggled without pleasure.

"Is Rudi here?"

"Rudi," she said. "I do not know where Rudi is. I only talk to him on the telephone."

"Do you know why I'm here?"

"No."

"But I'm supposed to meet somebody?"

"No." She giggled again. "Somebody supposed to meet *you*."

"I don't understand."

"Somebody supposed to look at you, identify you. *You* are not supposed to do anything, except be with me at a quarter after twelve. Here we are. And now it is half after twelve."

"Is there somebody here now?"

"Maybe he left already. I do not know which one it is. This kind of party, anybody comes, any reason. I tell Rudi when a party is, and he uses it the way he wants. I do not know who he will send. I only know you must be careful of Rudi."

Sand sat up on the bed, then made it to his feet. He helped Sara to a standing position. "Let's get some air," he said.

"We go to my place," Sara said. "We may as well make love as do something else." Again she was matter-of-fact, not even cynical.

"And how about Rudi?"

"Rudi. I will tell you about this Rudi."

They crossed the outer room toward the hall. There was a silence in the place, though the people were still there, and a haze that settled over the still forms like smoke upon a ruin. Down on the street, they wandered through the maze, coming out at last opposite the Jardin de Luxembourg. They traversed the boulevard and entered the rue Monsieur le Prince. In a little while he was helping her upstairs in a narrow building, relieved in his conviction that Rudi would not be here, had probably never set foot in the place, and had little interest in who did.

"So you see what sort of man this is," Sara was saying. She had been mumbling about Rudi all the way from the party. "That's why I told you be careful. I do not know what you are doing. But I never know Rudi to do nothing without some-thing in it that I don't approve. And when *I* do not approve, that is already something, I promise you."

Sand took her key and opened the door to the shabby room. It had a loose air of permanent negligence, and a bed that from the looks of it had never been made. Sara Gleize went directly to a cupboard and took out a bottle of cheap brandy, which she brought with her to the bed.

"All those weeks," she said, "sneaking about in that Hotel Victoire, and afterward too, living in that old *bordel* up there, my dear Rudi is telling me how hard he search every day for a solution to our problems and a good position. How did I know he cannot get an honest job even if he wishes to, not without papers, not in Paris. And that was his excuse, later on, but first I think he did not know it himself. He was just afraid, trying to fool everybody, even me. He did not look for a position. He did not do anything. All he did was sit on a bench in the Tuileries all day and cry, and whistle at the girls when he gets bored of crying. I know, because his stories were silly after a while, and I began to follow him. He is just a little boy playing games, Rudi is, with all those black suits and mys-teries, and it was only time before he gets into his old ways again.

"What's he up to now?" Sand asked. He was staring out into a faceless inner court, trying to picture a fat, tearful Rudi in the Tuileries.

"I do not know. Anything that comes along, I think. He has some business getting American cars from Denmark into Spain—it was all mixed up with the Geneva currency ex-change. Then he has a trade in American passports. That did not last. Now he does a little of everything, and controls peo-ple. He is not a fool, that Rudi, he gets his fingers into all the soups, and there are some lovely soups in Europe these days. And one of the best is this information-peddling, to the embassies and undergrounds. Maybe you are mixed up with that one, who knows?"

Sara glanced at him without interest, seemingly surprised that he was in her room, as if she'd noticed him for the first time. "Have a drink," she said politely, flourishing the bottle. She was still a pretty girl, much thinner now, with curious red-black hair, white skin, and Slavic features. She offered him a coquettish smile, more out of habit, he felt, than desire. When he remained at the window, she shrugged her shoulders and went on talking, rambling, bitter, plaintive, her thickened voice losing half the words into her pillow.

Sand listened to how Rudi had left her, had simply disappeared for weeks, and returned a wealthy citizen of Egypt. He was making provision for her too, he had said, and at last they would be married. But she knew he had done nothing for her at all, and would not marry her, and she decided the time had come to leave him. She had borrowed a little money, enough for this room, and left him her address in case he wanted to get hold of her. Now she worked as an artist's model in the rue de la Grande Chaumière, and did odd jobs for Rudi when he needed a woman for a particular purpose or, she implied to Sand, a particular client.

And before sinking into a stupor of misery, she raised her head and looked Sand in the face. "You may think," she said, "that I am in a bad position to criticize Rudi. But I never know much better life than I am living now. I am not of good family like him, I am not intelligent like him. I was a prostitute when he found me and a prostitute when he left me. I am a prostitute now—" She looked at Sand and shook her head. "You were a friend to us, I am not asking *you* for anything, only kindness. But it is a funny thing about Rudi. He is not really a bad man or, I should say, a bad little boy, for he is still a little boy. Only he blinds himself to what he is doing so long as he can play his games and pretend he is fooling people.

Otherwise he cries. And another funny thing, he has never liked any women but prostitutes. He likes to dirty himself, Rudi. He is not healthy. But what I blame him for only is persuading me to take that dance-hall job in Prague, for the money and information it would bring him, and the new black suit. He told me, you see, that if I did not report these people, somebody else would, and so it did not matter. He said that there is no right on either side—it is every man for himself in the modern world, he told me, and I was weak enough to listen to this. And I must live with what I did, and, even worse, I go on doing it for him here." Sara was crying quietly. "You see, I am still in love with him, with the gentleman in him, with the Gleize family which was friend to the great Presidents. At the same time I hate him; I would kill him if I am stronger. Can you understand me, Barney? I love him and I would like him dead. He is the bad habit that gives pleasure, then weakness, and then death." Her eyes closed, and in a moment the bottle slid from her fingers and the brandy poured out across the flimsy rug upon the floor.

Eyes still closed, she reached for it, but her fingers, yellow with nicotine, slipped weakly on the dark green glass of the empty bottle, which rolled away beneath her bed. Still she searched for it, fingers groping through gray balls of dust. Sand was conscious of her effort but paralyzed by the inertia of its hopelessness. He made no attempt to help her.

"It's empty," he muttered finally.

The hand stopped moving on the floor. Then she rolled over very slowly and stared at him and started to shake her head, saying, "No, Barney, no, Barney, no. You stay away from Rudi, keep away from him; no matter what he tells you, don't believe it—please, Barney, please. In some way he is selling you, do you understand? He sells everything, my Rudi—it is all he knows how to do—and it is no difference if what he is selling is not his." She was still shaking her head, back and forth, back and forth, against the rumpled pillow. "One time I dreamed I was searching for him, and on a corner somewhere in the world I found him. He had a little kiosk, and he was selling lives. In his hands they looked like artificial flowers. And I said, 'Rudi, sell me back my life and I will go away forever,' and he said, 'You come too late, it is already sold, your little life.' And I said, 'Who did you sell it to,' and he said, 'I sell it to myself, I wear it in my lapel.' And I looked and saw it hanging there, so old and faded."

She closed her eyes again and started to laugh, then stopped, weakly proffering her hand. "Lie down with me, Sand, be kind with me." But there was no desire in that face of youth and infinite defeat, and he could not take advantage of her offer, of her cynicism.

"What are you doing, Sand, what are you going to do?"

But Sara's voice trailed away again, and the hand fell, and her love was lost to him, and his to her. She was unconscious. He bent and kissed the pallid skin and went away.

8

Lise met him, troubled, at the door, and he greeted her warmly and laughed at her innuendoes about his absence overnight. Yet she took more than casual interest in the possibility of a love affair, and a touch of her fingers to his throat set off a restless beating in his heart. But he was surprised when, the very next day, she brought him his breakfast in bed. She wore her bathrobe with her usual negligence, but was fresh and carefully made-up, and she set down the tray before him in a manner that presented her perfume and her breasts to excellent advantage.

"Olivier had to go out early," she said, sighing, "and I feel lonely. I wanted to have breakfast with somebody, and you weren't up yet. You aren't angry, Bar-ney, that I've awakened you?" Until this morning, she had always called him Sand.

He shook his head, and she sank gracefully to the edge of the bed and gazed at him. Lise's serene, semi-smiling innocence was arch, and at first he resented her, for himself and for Olivier. At the same time he wanted her badly and was unable to stifle a certain exultation when she smoothed in advance the path of his approach. For over their coffee, sighing, whispering in turn, she confessed what he had long since guessed, that she and Olivier were not married, that she would never marry, since she felt that love should be spontaneous, an expression of happiness shared with another person. She and Jacobi—but here she paused to vent that too-rich sigh of melancholy rapture peculiar to French women.

"Love," she breathed after a moment. "There are times when it seems as inevitable as air."

This piece of foolishness was too much for Sand, but his impulse to drive her away from the bed was subdued easily by the warmth of her thigh against his own. Upset and irritated with himself, he took her hand, a gesture she hastened to interpret as an act of love. She bent immediately and pressed her lips into his neck, as if overcome despite herself by such virility.

"What are we up to?" he inquired of her ear, and her cheek drew back against his own. Why, she's grinning like a goddam hyena, he thought, and fought to repress an angry laugh.

"Are your intentions honorable, *Monsieur le Duc?*" Her whisper teased the corner of his mouth.

"No," he snapped, "they're too dishonorable even for me." Yet he found himself too aroused to push her away.

Lise stiffened at his words, then slowly sat up. She watched him a moment, then shrugged her shoulders. "*Adieu,*" she whispered enigmatically, and placing jam on a piece of croissant, popped it into her mouth.

And seeing her eyes, he knew their moment had come and gone, that she was his no longer. And he was honest enough to realize that, regardless, he had betrayed Olivier, for her right and wrong were not his own. He had ceded his conscience, as it proved, for nothing.

"Jacobi," Lise reflected aloud, as if comparing his attitude favorably with Sand's, "I remember—"

"Where did you know Jacobi, anyway?" Sand demanded, shifting restlessly in the bed.

He glared as, chewing placidly on one croissant, then another, and interrupting herself from time to time to sigh ro-
mantically, nod philosophically, and lick jam from her
fingertips, she recounted the details of her affair with Jacobi—
the most remarkable event, she impressed upon Sand, in her
life, if not, indeed, in the recorded history of mankind. She
had memorized every moment of it, real or imagined, and re-
lived them aloud in a voice of such dramatic timbre as to move
herself to tears and set the croissant crumbs to trembling on
her nether lip.

It appeared that Jacobi, after leaving Perpignan in 1938,
had journeyed west along the Pyrenees to the Atlantic coast,
where he rejoined Marat at Hendaye. There they had awaited
a third man, in the house of Marat's friend, Olivier, near the
beach.

Marat himself had crossed the frontier from Spain with
the help of Basque smugglers of the region who operated
across the mountain passes and by sea, in blue tuna boats out
of Saint-Jean-de-Luz. They controlled as well a certain minor
traffic back and forth across the river mouth, between the
clam-diggers on both sides. Mingling on the tidal flats of the
river delta, they dealt in petty objects beneath the noses of
the frontier guards at Fuenta Arabia.

These diggers would lend their skiffs to Marat, who, with
Jacobi, would row up the quiet Irgun River toward the foot-
hills, in case their comrade was marooned somewhere along
the Spanish bank. This was unlikely, since the sentinel sta-
tions were scarcely a hundred yards apart, and the river was
so narrow that even a wounded man could swim it if he wished
to risk a shot, but it gave them something to do. And they
would go sometimes in the tuna boats, fishing gradually south
during the day and moving in off the Spanish shore at night,
to pick up refugees. The fishermen made a profitable double
business, landing refugees on the steep coast above Hendaye

on their way home to Saint-Jean-de-Luz. There was a beach there, hidden beneath the cliff, and Jacobi took to visiting it in the daytime.

Lise at that time was engaged to Olivier and was staying with him at Hendaye. Olivier himself worked most of the day at his sculpture. Marat disliked the beach. He preferred to lounge indoors and read aloud—to himself if nobody else was there to listen—or write dramatic manifestoes on various subjects pertaining to the Party. Marat's voice was the prevailing force in the house, and a source of annoyance to everybody but himself.

As for Jacobi, he had resented Lise at first, content to go by himself down the long sand of Hendaye and around the broken point where two rock towers stood apart from shore, and across the tide pools and warm flat boulders into the cove at one end of his own beach. When the tide was high there was a second route he liked as well, up over the sea fields that sloped to the edge of the cliff. One could lie there in the cool spring grass and stare straight down into a narrow grotto where the waves, sweeping in from the Atlantic, would plunge with a roar of self-destruction, sending their bright spray high in the air above the field of flowers. After crossing the point, he could descend to the beach down a long precipitous sandbank studded with crippled cypress, and there remove his clothes and swim to the rock island. The island protected his clumsy stroke from the motion of the sea, and he would rest on it, fresh from the cold June water. After those years in Spain, Lise said, nodding her head as one who knew, he badly needed this repose.

It disturbed her slightly that he took no more pleasure in the company of the others, herself included. They seemed to annoy him and make him nervous, especially in their amusements. And because he could not seem to find companionship among them, he retreated into solitude. Even

Marat, his one friend, if he had a friend, whom he had sol-
diered with in Spain—even Marat, with the war and the
cause at a distance, now seemed to irritate him. How easily
had Marat cast away that heavy chain of months—this observation Lise recalled having been confided to herself—how
readily had he dismissed each link of their defeat with dialectics. Dialectics were changeable, expedient, Jacobi had
remarked, politically useful, no doubt, but then, politics were
not truly his concern.

Whereas Marat mouthed words, tasted them like a con-
noisseur, and when Jacobi pointed out their contradictions
would only roar with laughter. "That's the beauty of them!"
he would shout, and clap his sullen friend across the shoulders. "You're a bourgeois at heart, *mon capitaine Jacobi*, you're
behind the times, you're not at all adaptable, *mon vieux*."

But Marat, at worst, was only cynical. Jacobi respected him
as a soldier and did not question the man's usefulness to the
Party. But Olivier—He made no secret of his contempt for
this gentle, uncommitted man, who paid lip service to Jacobi's
own ideals and to the Party, yet whose doubt about the means
tainted every question, every attitude. The Party, Jacobi felt,
had no place for such people. Yet Marat claimed that every
man might in the end be useful, and though he conceded that
Olivier would probably forsake the Party before very long—
we intellectuals, Lise averred, were forced by conscience to
quit the Party in 1939—he was clearly very fond of him. Or,
at least, he was amused by him, for Marat let fly his maniacal
laughter every time Olivier opened his mouth, while Jacobi
would only frown and crack his knuckles.

Lise, of course, was devoted to Olivier and amused by him,
but she felt a kinship with Jacobi in that she did not entirely
share the constant nonsense of the other two. Like Jacobi, she
felt obliged to glance from Olivier to Marat and back, as if in

this way she might creep closer to the source of their amusement and have some of its warmth. Unlike Jacobi, she would
finally find something to laugh at, and then he would gaze at
her for several moments with those very cold black eyes, as if
she were some sort of disagreeable exhibit.

Here Lise paused, in awe of her own evocation. Sand was
touched by her artlessness, her impulsive vulnerability, and
the big, generous tongue that seized on this moment of silence
to venture out in search of croissant crumbs. Her soft moist
brown eyes seemed no match for those eyes of Jacobi, deep
black, and bright as lenses. And yet in her way, with that
spongy resilience of innocence, she was invincible.

Jacobi was deeply attracted to her, Lise remarked, hurrying
back to her favorite theme. So was Marat. Marat never missed
a chance to lay his hands on her, and flaunted his intent before Olivier, yet all but Jacobi were aware that his overtures
would come to nothing. Jacobi watched them in silence, condemning Olivier for permitting such liberties to Marat, and
staying away from her as much as possible. There was something of the puritan about Jacobi—or so it seemed to Lise,
who could not otherwise account for his reserve in her direction. She recalled with remarkable precision those details of
her person and appearance that contributed to the rout of that
reserve, though needless to say she had not had the slightest
notion of encouraging him.

One afternoon, having nothing better to do, she went for
a walk over the cliffs, in the direction of his beach. From high
above she could see Jacobi at the water's edge. He had started
to undress. She was wearing, she recalled, a quite pretty blue
frock, silhouetted against her by the summer wind. When,
glancing up, he saw her, she waved to him, then pretended to
turn away, having no wish to intrude.

In answer he pointed at his own route down the bank and

came slowly to meet her at the bottom. She arrived scratched and breathless, laughing; but he did not laugh in return. "What are you doing here?" he asked.

She cocked her head, a little hurt. "I'm sorry," she said. "I was just out for a walk."

"It's all right," he said.

"Obviously it isn't." She started back up the slope, but he came after her and took her hand. "I'm sorry," he said. "You took me by surprise."

She descended again, and they walked along the beach.

"You like it out here, don't you?" Lise said. "By yourself, I mean."

"Yes," he said. Jacobi was not shy, but a solitary man, out of practice in making conversation. Finally he said, "Did you bring your bathing suit?"

"No," she said. "Isn't that stupid? I was in such a hurry that I forgot! And now I'm much too lazy to go back." She looked at him. "But you go ahead; I'll watch."

"I haven't got one either," he said. "I don't usually need one."

"Go ahead anyway, I don't mind. I'll turn my head if you like."

He shook his head. "I don't have to swim," he said.

"You Americans!" she teased him. "Look, I'll make a bargain with you. We'll both go."

"Naked?"

"In our underthings."

"And Olivier?"

"Why should he care? I'm over twenty; you must be nearly forty. We're not virgins any more; we've got nothing to hide from each other." She laughed at him, kicking off her shoes.

"All right," Jacobi said. The decision made, he undressed quickly to his shorts and waited for her at the edge of the water. "Do you want to swim to the island?" he asked, trying not to look at her.

"Let's." She ran past him into the water—rather gracelessly, she recalled, since her hips even then were much too full (at this point Lise rose from the bed and did a pirouette for Sand, who obligingly denied it), wearing panties and brassière, and the panties became transparent as she started to swim.

He knew she knew they were transparent, and that he was watching her motion in the water, and was rather self-conscious for this reason. Then, for the first time in her life, she heard Jacobi laugh. It was a mirthless laugh, and it upset her. On the island before him, she sat with her back to him, clutching her knees to her chest. He climbed out and lay down and watched her. Her back was brown and sparkling with water drops, but his gaze kept returning to a white line of flesh above the panties.

"The water's cold," she said. "It makes me tingle."

"Yes," he said. They stared out across the sea-smoothed rocks at the quiet ocean.

"It's peaceful," she said.

"Yes," he said. And as if to distract himself, he described to her the other side of the Atlantic, the fishing and swimming and sailing enjoyed by all Americans, talking on and on with the breathless enthusiasm of a boy. When she interrupted, he lost the thread of what he was saying, so disturbed was he by the profile of her body. He fixed his eyes determinedly on her face, which at that time was really quite handsome in a natural sort of way. In those days, Lise confided, her cheeks were round and rosy, and her smile displayed a pair of dimples quite well known in the area.

Here Lise paused to giggle happily at her own vanity, and as her smile chanced to fall upon the lucky Sand, who lay now with his hands behind his head, the devastating dimples were revealed to him. A moment before, he had been struck and saddened by the realization that Jacobi's Atlantic coast, described so enthusiastically to Lise, was none other than Sand's own, as if the man had had no pleasant memories to draw upon, and knew happiness only secondhand. The dimples intruded on these reflections, and at first Sand pretended not to notice. But Lise smiled on, relentless. Embarrassed for her, he saluted the dimples with exaggerated compliments until she pinched him, delighted. Then he smiled to himself maliciously, for where one of the dimples should have been there clung instead a bit of butter.

Lise had resumed her account of her interlude with Jacobi, and was frowning in order to convey the seriousness of their discussion.

"You're a strange man," she told him, "but not at all as Marat describes you. He says you are ruthless, harsh, that you find no horror in killing people."

"One gets hardened to everything sooner or later. I haven't had time to give myself much thought in these past years."

"Perhaps you come out here alone to think about it."

"Perhaps I do." He watched her as she entered the water. She turned and caught him watching, he had no time to dissemble, and they both laughed quietly, swimming together toward shore.

"It's been too long, I'm afraid," he muttered, and she answered, "Poor man," with sympathy, but did not encourage him further. They dressed with their backs to each other and went on up the sandbank to the field.

In the light of late afternoon the headland was very beautiful. From the cliff edge, where they stood, they gazed at the huge château on the hill to the east, at the dark green Pyrenees with their hint of rainbow to the south, to the far coast of Spain and the Atlantic, blue black, north and west. The

light was dramatic, as in a Romantic landscape, and Lise, remarking on it, exclaimed, "Poussin, or Watteau! Yes, that's it,
'The Departure for Cythera.'" She saw that Jacobi did not
understand. "It's a painting," she explained, "too good to be
true, unreal. Cythera was Aphrodite's island, a paradise. Now
and again, for a brief moment like this, we get a glimpse of it
on earth."

But he only stared at her, and she was not certain he had
understood.

They were going home across the headland, through the
wild flowers in the sea field. Lise bent to pick them, and as
Jacobi watched her, sank down among them and closed her
eyes. "It's really too perfect," she murmured. "I have to savor
it a moment."

He stood above her, hands in pockets, then swiftly kneeled
beside her. He made love to her. He was out of his senses,
moving through a dream, and though she resisted him she
could not stop him, and he would have taken her by force if
it had come to that, but it did not. In the end she succumbed
as well as he, and held to him fervently until twilight came,
when she began to cry.

He was standing again, gazing down upon her. "I'm
sorry," he said, angry and ashamed. "If you wish, you can
tell Olivier that I attacked you." Jacobi had a tooth-for-tooth
sense of justice and thought that this way she might revenge
herself. And for her sake he added, "You'd only be telling
the truth."

"That's not so," she whispered. "No, no, no, I am crying
only because I am a hypocrite, Jacobi." She indicated the fad-
ing scene around them with a disconsolate wave of her hand.
"It was wonderful, wasn't it? Cythera. You mustn't take that
away from me as well."

They walked on slowly, a distance between them, struggling to assimilate the experience. At the house they met Oli-

vier, and became strangers, far apart. Jacobi left the following morning for Paris and America.

"And I have never seen him since." Lise sighed, tears welling in her eyes, as if in this sad circumstance lay the story of a broken life.

"You didn't know him very long, then, did you?" Sand reminded her unkindly, impatient to get out of bed, to go to a café alone and piece together these new clues.

Lise whirled on him, outraged. "Time is no measure of a love such as ours!" she cried with a hauteur intended to convey the distinction in her mind between the forceful Jacobi on the sea cliffs of long ago and the lackluster youth crouched back among the covers.

"But you see, Lise," Sand said after a moment, stung, "I am Olivier's friend, and Jacobi was not."

She knew precisely what he meant and was, in fact, overwhelmed by the new drama—a lover's sacrifice on the altar of pure friendship—*magnifique!* Tears flew to her eyes once more, and embracing him passionately, as if in final parting, she whispered, "Dear Bar-ney, you are right, we must not think only of ourselves. For Jacobi it was another matter, but for us—"

And, dissolved in noble grief, she fled the room, securing an orange from the table on the way.

Sand lay laughing quietly in bed. But his laugh was soon angry and ended in a snort of impatience. He sat up violently. He was frustrated, and annoyed with Lise; but, more than that, he sensed a new objectivity toward Jacobi, this Jacobi who could and did despise a gentle creature like Olivier, who could and did take Lise by force—what sort of man was that? And he didn't want to be objective yet, nor until his search was over. It was one thing to seek someone in vain, quite another to go on seeking in the knowledge that that someone was unworthy of the search. He shrugged the thought away, like cold.

For Jacobi it was another matter, Lise had said. But was it really, was the man so different, then, from everybody else? Or was it that people, even people like his father—yes, and Lise, who had small reason to be grateful to Jacobi—were anxious to accord him the benefit of every doubt. Sand did himself, and always had. And why?

He wanted more than ever now to see the man again.

9

The rain came down and down and down, and the days ran together like dirty water drops across the window.

Sand felt caged in his proximity to Lise, who, used to him now, was casual in her dress and ways and treated him in all but one respect as if he were Olivier. He sat at the table, waiting, glaring at the wall.

The man named Marat was clearly in no hurry to see him. Rudi had all but disappeared. And Jacobi. The journals, including those serviced by Sand's own agency, had now assumed, proclaimed, that he was dead, and the Party had not denied it in its usual violent manner, but said only, in a small official announcement, that members should pay no attention, for Jacobi was alive. It neither denied nor confirmed an alteration in his status. But Lise, among others, was certain the man was dead.

"They are only seeking an excuse for announcing it to the rank and file; they cannot simply depose a man as popular as that without a good explanation." Her voice broke with anger. "I am afraid you are waiting for nothing, my dear friend."

And Sand could not help agreeing with her. But still he

waited, day after day, unable to believe that Rudi would not come and let him know. He did not want to believe that Rudi himself didn't know, and was avoiding him.

But one night Olivier was waiting when he came in. "You must get some rest," Olivier said. "We are leaving in the morning."

"Where are we going?"

"I am taking you to Marat," Olivier said.

"And then what? Do I wait again?" Sand sat down and slowly shook his head.

"I don't know," Olivier said, quite miserable in his inability to comfort. He sat there all the night with Sand, who, half asleep, refused to go to bed. In the morning he was weak and tired, and Olivier was forced to guide him down the stairs.

It was cold in the streets, the first harsh day of October, and the air and the pale sunlight awakened Sand to his mission. He saw that Olivier was carrying his bag, and realized he had not said good-by to Lise. Angry with himself, he blurted out, "Where are we going?"

And Olivier smiled at him and said again, "I am taking you to Marat."

They were walking down the Quai des Grands Augustins toward Saint-Michel, and passed a pink building which Sand, to his dismay, perceived was tilted out over the street. He pomted it out to Olivier, who laughed and said, "No, you are not seeing things, and look, I will show you something." He led Sand to a ground-floor window and indicated a large unfinished figure in white marble. "It is a Rodin," he whispered, "a real one. Just sitting there all by itself, with nobody to look at it or care for it." He shook his head. "But the building is really tilted, yon know; you are not seeing things." He turned to Sand and put his arm across his shoulder. "Not that you should believe everything you see, *mon cher,* you must judge carefully

for yourself." He led Sand across the bridge to the Ile de la
Cité and the flower market, a bright oasis in the shadow of
the Préfecture de Police.

Olivier was as welcome here as elsewhere, and he knew
most of the flower-sellers by name. He strode expansively up
and down the rows, strewing compliments and jokes, advising
customers, adjusting stems, and telling Sand about the bird
market, which replaced the flower show on Sundays.

"You have never seen such birds!" he exclaimed. "All
colors, shapes, and songs. Why, there are birds here which can
be seen no other place in the world! You doubt me, my dear
Sand? You say that it is impossible? Well, then, I will tell you
the secret. They *dye* these birds, a lot of them—and how is
one to tell? Take a filthy sparrow off the street, dip the little
fellow in a pot of paint, and what do you have? Why, you have
the priceless Crimson Nightingale, from the Kerguelen Islands, for only nine thousand francs the pair! And you must
only note, if you are naturally of a suspicious nature, that these
exotic creatures come from remote islands, where few have
ever been, and are so rare as to be omitted from even the
most comprehensive volumes of ornithology, and so delicate
that they barely chirp, and die within the week, as further
proof of authenticity. The dye is bad for Crimson Nightin-
gales, you see, and one must replace them once a week, at
only nine thousand francs the pair!" Olivier's voice was one
of mock astonishment, and he raised his eyebrows at the
flower-sellers as if they might share the guilt of their Sunday
brethren. "Why, I myself once purchased your beautiful
American Cardinal, but it moulted overnight, and when the
feathers came in again I recognized it immediately as a countryman, and put it back in the Jardin de Luxembourg where
it belonged."

Olivier laughed a little, despite his disapproval. "It is often
like that in Paris," he concluded. "The obvious beauty is so

often false, and the true beauty is hidden away from the world, like that Rodin statue we glimpsed a little while ago.

Sand nodded, groping for Olivier's point and its importance to his welfare. He recognized the other's kind intent in leading him here, in affording him a balancing force for whatever lay ahead. And he wanted to linger a little longer, absorbing the bright, warming colors of the flowers and the pure odor of their loam, reminiscent of days of faraway summer, shimmering in the distance of his memory. Among these cheerful faces, high-colored from the country, he fancied himself a part of a healthy pageant—he was one of them, a man among other men. He wanted to stroll back down the banks of plants, and listen to Olivier and the laughter in their wake, and feel identified with joy again, as Olivier had guessed he needed. And he wanted to clasp Olivier's hand and get across to him how much his friendship meant.

Instead they turned from the flower market and went away around the corner, where the city opened out again, its reality gray beneath the high façade of Notre Dame. Drab pigeons swirled the sooty air and landed, grumbling, and from the meager trees along the quai the yellow leaves fell silently, relentlessly.

"Olivier, tell me," Sand said, pausing. "What is your frank opinion of Jacobi?"

"My frank opinion is not necessarily an honest one." Olivier, who had been singing to himself, lifted his shoulders in a heavy shrug. "One must respect a creature of the sort, but one is not forced to like him."

"You do respect him, though."

"Well, in a way I do. I have the feeling, though, that if I were a less ordinary man perhaps I wouldn't. Jacobi appeals to the ordinary man because he has the courage to be honest and unselfish to the point of ruthlessness. He says and does precisely what he believes, he stands up to authority, majorities, anything that gets in his way. For that reason he is a sort of folk hero, even to people who disagree with everything about him, like myself. I suppose people need to feel that man is capable of any action he believes in, and cling to the few who are. And, however he got that way, Jacobi is no fanatic and no fraud. But for all these reasons, and because he has no humor, he is dangerous. He is too strong for other men to live with, tolerate, which is why, like all strong creatures, he is punished for his strength when he grows weak."

They were walking on across the Place de Notre-Dame. "Jacobi is rare even in the Party," Olivier continued, musing. "There are other incorruptibles—many of them—but they are largely uneducated men among the rank and file. Then there are the incorruptibles like me, who are treated with contempt by all the others." Olivier laughed aloud. "We joined because we hated world injustice, because we were emotional and sensitive. We are the ones who quit with a scream of disenchantment. Then there are the Marats, the theorists. They are often the revolutionary fanatics, and are almost always neurotic in some way, or frauds. I don't think Marat is a fanatic, but he is certainly a fraud, which is why I prefer him to Jacobi—I can understand a fraud, he shares our mortal failings." Olivier laughed again. "Why, Marat's name isn't Marat at all; he is really of the nobility. He suffers from the guilt of wealth, like so many of their theorists. But he's a man of the people now, clothes, accent, and all. He's brilliant, which Jacobi is not, and he's courageous, and he has humor."

"Don't most people?"

"Not in the Party, I'm afraid. They take themselves too seriously. The workers are all right, the Party is only a sort of church for them, but the rest—well, they're apt to be misfits for the most part, especially the women. My God, they're an ugly lot, those Party women! I kept feeling that that was why they were in the Party in the first place, that was their grudge,

And those swarms of eager little men were stupefying—they all looked constipated or something.

"Not Marat, though," Olivier concluded. "He's most persuasive." This last remark held a note of warning that his smile did not conceal.

They returned to the Left Bank across the bridge that led to Saint-Julien-le-Pauvre. The quarter was old and cramped, unfamiliar to Sand, who, trailing Olivier along its narrow sidewalks, suffered a first feeling of entering an impasse. He felt trapped some minutes later when Olivier paused on a corner and turned to him, hand outstretched.

"Well, we are here, I'm afraid," he said ambiguously, and placed his other hand on Sand's tense shoulder. He nodded at the shop front of a bookstore so littered with posters and announcements of all kinds that its dark interior was scarcely visible. "You will ask them for Marat," Olivier said. "Good luck to you."

Sand said nothing in response, but watched his friend move away around the corner. "Good-by," he called then, "thanks very much"; but there was no answer, and he turned in time to glimpse a face observing him through the littered window of the shop. Its eyes turned away, and two hands appeared above the window sill, adjusting magazines.

10

Alone on the windy corner with his suitcase, Sand fought an impulse to retreat, and drove himself to the door of the shop. Its handle did not work, but spun aimlessly in his hand. Then the door opened from the inside, and a cat stepped out and rubbed itself against his leg. Its master, a gaunt, mournful man in a green turtle-neck sweater, waited in silence for Sand to speak. His hollowed face wore a suffering expression that seemed self-conscious, and even his pants and sweater had an affected air of poverty, more torn than filthy, more wrinkled than worn.

"Monsieur Marat?" Sand said.

"No," the man said, glancing up and down the street for no apparent reason, then stepping back behind the door. "Come in," he added in a voice thick with tragedy and significance, and a cold in the head.

Behind Sand the door closed quietly, and the man said, "Marat comes here once a day. Do you want to wait for him?" But he seemed to know that Sand had little choice in the matter, for he motioned him to a seat atop some books without waiting for an answer and disappeared through a narrow aperture in the rear of the room. There came the sound of stifled voices, like the passage of rats in the wainscoting, and

then there was silence. Sand, lighting a cigarette, was startled
by the sound of the match.

He took advantage of his solitude to inspect the place. Its
inside was a rag-tag heap of disarranged books, magazines, and
pamphlets flowing out of makeshift shelves onto makeshift
chairs and benches, topped here and there with dirty coffee
cups, ashtrays, and oddments of all kinds. The window was
devoted to posters announcing art exhibitions, political rallies,
and mixed opinions on the state of the world, almost all of
which were outdated. It permitted just enough light to read
by if one leaned toward it. There was, besides, a light bulb
naked on the ceiling, but it was brown with insects, and its
glow so feeble that one could not tell before twilight whether
it burned or not. The room itself, much too small for its con-
tents, seemed a barricade of momentous ideologies now shot
to pieces and left for dead by the world without. Its books and
pamphlets, though concerned with modern politics, fretted
over the contradictions of day to day. Each canceled out the
rest, and the effect of the entire collection was one of too-
early antiquity, a waste of confetti in empty avenues when the
parade has gone.

The inhabitants of the inner room, where he ventured late
that afternoon, sat in darkness like dusty moths, as if dependent for their nourishment on the hoard of mental refuse
cached around them. Sand had come to inquire after Marat,
and the shopkeeper said, "Marat wants very much to see you;
he will come before too long." He did not reveal the source
of this information, or offer further conversation. Sand stood
for a moment, at a loss. His eyes were adapting to the gloom,
and he saw a kerosene stove, a littered desk, and two iron cots,
and smelled human company long before he made it out. They
materialized one by one, four of them in all, in various pos-
tures upon the cots, yet he could not locate another door
through which they might come and go.

"We take turns on the cots," the shopkeeper muttered, and fingered his thin wrist. He presented three men and a girl, who, in the gloom, was only distinguishable from the emaciated men in that she did not need a shave. "This is Monsieur Sand," the shopkeeper said, thereby revealing his knowledge of Sand's identity, and the girl vented a small sound vaguely reminiscent of laughter.

Sand returned to the front of the shop and waited. But Marat did not come that evening, nor the next day, nor the next, and on the fourth day Sand lost heart and prepared to leave. He was rumpled and dirty from sleeping on a bench, and sick of the greasy bites he had gulped down twice a day in a nearby café, and angry at the refusal of these strange people to have anything to do with him. But the shopkeeper seemed to guess his intent, appearing suddenly with a cup of coffee for his guest. Sand sat down tiredly and sipped at the coffee, which was thick and cold and had too much sugar in it, and wondered what was happening to him.

He knew now that it was only to stave off an early admission of failure that he had come at all. Hadn't he realized even before leaving Olivier that Jacobi was lost to him? And even if Jacobi was not dead, what possible reason could the Party have for awarding him, Sand, an admitted representative of the Western press, an interview? And Marat. He could not even be sure that such a man existed, and if he did, then what was the delay, why did they keep him waiting everywhere? It seemed to Sand that he had been duped, led up a blind alley and deserted, for there was no logic anywhere in the picture. Yet he could not reconcile this decision with his knowledge of Rudi Gleize, who did not act without a purpose, and with the affirmation of Marat's existence by Lise and Olivier—though of course they might be part of the conspiracy. But then, what would make them all take so much trouble? He had no choice but to wait a little longer, to wait, to wait, as it now seemed to him he had waited all his life: for graduation from school, for enlistment in the army, for combat that never came, for the war to end, for college to end, for promotion in two jobs he did not want, for a love that did not exist—waiting for a raison d'être which never arrived because he could not recognize it.

Fighting self-doubt, he would curse himself aloud and leap to his feet like a man afraid of freezing in his sleep. Then he would wander to the window, and from the dirtied, dim reflection of his face, wan, hollow-eyed, irresolute against the background of the street and of the world, draw the angry self-contempt that kept him going.

Then Marat came. Sand did not recognize him at first, though he had been certain he would know him immediately. The man entered the shop early in the morning and sat himself down among the books opposite Sand, who was very much aware of him, not only because customers here were so very rare, but because the man himself was of such bizarre appearance. He was very tall and thin, with a huge crest of wild black hair, a blind eye that stared upward at the ceiling, a right nostril scarred and narrower than the left, and a very wide mouth which hung in a sort of smile. His expression, ferocious, was underlined by a thin black beard.

The man seemed quite conscious of his own appearance, for, catching Sand staring at him, he burst into raucous laughter and shouted out, "You look like you'd seen the devil incarnate, but you haven't, you know, it's another wretch just like yourself!" He eyed Sand's confusion with cool belligerence, and for the rest of that day observed with pointed interest every movement Sand made, so that the latter was ill at ease despite himself, and smoked too many cigarettes. Under this stranger's gaze his position appeared to Sand more pre-

posterous than ever. He could not concentrate on the Party
text he had been reading and finally was forced to meet the
other's stare.

Unlike those of the shopkeeper, the man's clothes were
worn and clean. He had a loud blue woolen scarf and a cor-
duroy jacket and even a complete set of buttons. But his skin
was stale with bad food, and his hair dull and damp, and his
eye too bright. Sand guessed that the privation was his own
doing, less asceticism than lack of interest, but not the result
of straitened means. The man's wild appearance might be affected, but not entirely so. He seemed to radiate a feverish
energy, to be constantly on the point of leaping into action of
some extraordinary dimension, which might end with a shout
of laughter, an obscene curse, a blow, the choice dependent
on a whim no average man could understand. Yet he only
crouched there, watching Sand, until finally the latter felt
compelled to say, "Is there something I can do for you?" He
still did not realize he was facing Marat.

"Yes," the other said delightedly, as if this were just what
he had waited for. But he gave no explanation, and finally
Sand said, "Perhaps you would tell me what it is?"

"No, I won't," the stranger retorted. "It's none of your
business." His face darkened with displeasure, then cleared
again. "Do you understand what you are reading?" he asked
Sand.

"I think so. It deals with the Party."

"It's out of date. You're wasting your time. Here, read this
instead." The man sprang to his feet and rooted furiously into
the pile of books he had been sitting on, scattering them all
over the room, and coming up at last with a single volume.
He held it for a moment in his hands, then tossed it violently
at Sand, who caught it clumsily against his chest. The stranger
stalked out of the shop.

He returned the next morning. "What did you think of the book?" he said to Sand.

"A lot of it seems self-evident," Sand admitted. "I mean, the idea that the people are being educated to expect more from life than mere existence and cannot be stopped from taking it. There can't be much quarrel with that."

"Of course there can. Haven't you heard that the people's rebellion is encouraged and exploited by the Party for political purposes?" The big face twisted sardonically.

"I don't think politics have too much to do with it. The principle is true of the poor in every country, it has nothing to do with nations, not at base."

The other hurled himself backward onto a heap of books and stretched out flat, his head propped against the wall. He studied Sand for a moment before he said quite calmly, "You sound like poor old Jacobi. You are too stupid to have followed the political developments, you are still in the primer stage."

"And what are the political developments you think are so important, monsieur—I don't think you gave me your name."

"No, I didn't," the man said rudely.

"So Jacobi's crime is that, then? An interest in people rather than politics?"

"Crime? I said nothing about a crime." He smiled, placing clasped hands upon his stomach. "But he can't think any further than the people. The Party is international, and its plans are long-range. Jacobi is an obstructionist; his views are archaic." He smiled again. "Or so I've heard."

"You think that's sufficient reason to depose him, Monsieur Marat?" Sand was surprised by the calmness of his own voice, for the other's identity had occurred to him only a moment before.

"It's not a question of what *I* think, Monsieur Sand." Marat pronounced the name with irritation, sitting up, but made no

further reference to Sand's discovery, and continued to speak
as if nothing had changed in their relationship. "I have nothing to do with it." He made the confession an enigmatic one,
vaguely creditable to himself. "It happens that I was a very
close friend of Jacobi."

"*Was* a very close friend?"

"Yes."

"Does that mean he is dead?"

"No."

"You mean he has become an obstructionist, whatever that
means, and therefore you are no longer his friend."

"If you like."

"Perhaps you are afraid to be his friend?"

"If you like." Marat's voice was metallic, monotone. He
seemed to be thinking of something else.

"If you are not afraid, then may I ask what your opinion
is?"

"Yes, you may."

"But you won't tell me."

"You are very intelligent, Monsieur Sand, you learn very
quickly. You are also very tiresome." Marat rose and went to
the door.

Sand followed him onto the street. "Are you coming
back?" he asked.

"Of course," Marat said, contemptuous. "What would you
do otherwise, Monsieur Sand? Isn't it Marat you were looking
for?"

"Then why didn't you tell me who you were?"

"What does it matter what I call myself? Do you know
who I am either way?" Marat accepted Sand's silence as a
victory for himself and said, "Now why do you want to see
Jacobi?"

"I used to know him."

"I used to know all sorts of people."

"Well, I'm a newspaperman. It would be interesting to talk to him. And I have a personal interest too."

"I'm sure of it." Marat belched, more coarsely than seemed necessary. "All right, then," he said, "we'll let you see him." He seemed suddenly elated, and dismissed Sand's further attempts at conversation with impatient shrugs and grimaces, intent on some thought process of his own.

In the days that followed, however, nothing was done to bring Sand closer to Jacobi. Marat came and went infrequently, and the people in the shop took no more notice of Sand than they had before.

The wind outside made the window shake, and Sand watched the sky sink low over the litter of crouched buildings, as if it might founder of its own gray weight. Unlike the poor in Olivier's area, the people here were apathetic, spent, moving slowly down the street on quests which they appeared to know would come to nothing. He fretted dully, in abstract irritation. True, the search was going forward, step by uncertain step, but it was no longer under his own direction. He wondered if he had ever controlled it at all, or if he had only been controlled by it. He felt himself a prisoner, not of the bookshop, nor even of Marat, but of himself, of some fatuous diehard hope of man.

At the next chance he demanded of Marat, "What are you waiting for? Why did you have me come here?" and because he spoke so rarely these days his voice broke on a high note, as in alarm.

"The place is useful for making contacts, it is so anonymous. Why?" he inquired, whirling upon Sand. "Aren't you interested in these creatures here? They are fantastic. They lie in there waiting like so many sick cats to see which way to jump, and no matter which way the world goes will count for

nothing. They regard themselves as non-partisans, philoso-
phers, transcending the stinking strife, but they are lampreys
dragging from the people's belly, the filthiest of all filth!"

He jumped to his feet. "The people! Stinking, yes, but a
healthy stink, at least!" His voice had mounted to a shout, and
he shook his hands violently in Sand's face, as if he might
strangle him. "*I* am the people! Look at me, Sand, and remember! I am noisy and vulgar and stupid and shrewd, and I am
dangerous! I will not be denied; I am too strong, do you understand, too hungry! I am neither good nor bad, I have a
strong eye and a blind eye, white teeth and rotten breath,
a kind heart and a cruel spleen! I am god and devil, animal
and spirit, genius and bloody jackass! And I am capable of
anything, absolutely anything, so long as I am alive, do not
forget it!"

The outburst recalled Jacobi's harsh statement of faith, so
long ago in Perpignan, in that both men had become angry in
the process. But Jacobi had been prodded into speaking out,
whereas Marat had pounced upon an opportunity. Jacobi's anger, directed at society, had been spontaneous, whereas the
rage of Marat, if Olivier had been right about his ancestry,
seemed grandiloquent, a practiced piece of showmanship directed at Sand alone. Still, there was something of Jacobi here
in the tones and rhythms, the tense incantations of the
hands—with the difference that Marat, whatever the depth of
his feelings, enjoyed the role, even caricatured it.

Now he was glaring ferociously through the window,
breathing noisily and grinding his hands together. "Yes," he
muttered, "I think I will show you the people, and then you
will see. They are contemptible," he added, whirling to face
Sand once more, "but you will have contempt for them only
at your cost!"

"Why are you shouting at me?" Sand said. "I only asked
you why you brought me here. I want to know why you're

making me wait. Why don't we go straight to Jacobi and have done with it?"

"Never mind, never mind! I told you you'd see him, and you will!"

Sand wanted to ask, What's in this for the Party; what possible use am I to you? But he only said in irritation, "And I don't agree that the people are contemptible. We are all human animals together, in the end."

"Human animals! What do *you* know about human animals, an imbecile like you!" Marat was beside himself anew. "*I'll* show you human animals, *I'll* show you Jacobi's noble people, the real people, and then we'll see how smug you are, you parasite!" Marat ground his teeth in the passion of his fury, then burst into a roar of laughter without changing his expression. "We'll take a tour of Paris, lovely Paris, you and I. You'll find it edifying, I promise you."

"All right," Sand said. "When do we leave?"

Marat raised his eyebrows, mistaking Sand's bewilderment for complacency, but did not speak further. He answered Sand's question with laughter at the back of his throat before disappearing into the back room of the shop. From there he shouted, some moments later, the single word, "Tomorrow!"

11

Sand had no idea that from the very beginning of his search for Jacobi he had been followed. He found out through Marat, who returned for him that same evening after dark.

"I'll leave first," Marat said. "You wait ten minutes, then go out and take the first street to the right. At the corner go left, then left again, until you are back on this street, where, turning right, you will walk on slowly until I join you, understand?"

"I thought we were leaving tomorrow," Sand said.

"I know you did," Marat said. "That's why we're leaving tonight."

"Oh," Sand said. He spoke sarcastically, but he did not feel sarcastic. Marat's refusal that afternoon to say why they did not go straight to Jacobi had confirmed a new suspicion. Sara had been right, and he should have realized it from the start. Rudi Gleize had sold him to the Party, and the Party thought him important, for otherwise why would a man like Marat be assigned to him? As for making him wait, he thought, it must be a matter of timing. Clearly this timing had to be precise and, since they had waited so long, was probably dependent on some circumstance beyond their control. That cir-

cumstance was imminent now, and afterward—what became
of him afterward?

Marat eyed him from the doorway. "I'll be watching you,"
he said, "in case you become confused, my friend, and go in
the wrong direction."

Ten minutes, Sand thought. If I turn left and run—No,
I'm losing my nerve, I've got to get hold of myself. If only I
hadn't had to wait so long, had so much time to worry.

The swirling night, refracting the city lights, was misty
purple, like bad amethyst. He turned to the right and around
the block, as directed, and went on walking. This was a market
area, shuttered in iron. There were grilles on the shop windows, and heavy padlocks on the grilles. *Clip, clap, clip, clap,*
rang his heels, the sound imprisoned in the street. Barney
Sand—Paris, 1953, he thought, remembering his book, and
tried to smile. Over the door of a horse butcher a pigeon
perched on the gilt head of a horse and ruffled its feathers at
the fog, and far ahead of him toward the river a figure angled
out across an intersection and disappeared.

There was nothing behind him, nobody. But around the
next corner Marat waited, leaning on the side-street wall. He
beckoned to Sand, then seized his arm and led him swiftly
into a small bistro several doors beyond. They took a table in
the corner.

"Who is it?" Marat asked. They ordered calvados.

"Who?"

"Come on! He followed you around that block—part way
around, that is, because then he smelled the trap and went on
straight ahead." Marat drained his glass and wiped his open
mouth with the back of his big hand. "So you telephoned, did
you? Why did he come tonight?"

"I didn't telephone. Who'd want to follow me?"

Marat snapped a wedge of wax from the drippings of a
candle in a wine bottle. "What do you take us for, a pack of

idiots?" Yet he was not angry. He was smiling feverishly, excited, like a child absorbed in a game.

They spent the night there on two benches in a side room, rising before light and walking to the river and across a bridge that Sand had never seen. For days they wandered through the city, sleeping in cafés, theaters, prostitutes' hotels, and once in the hay of a farm truck that had broken down at the city markets. Wherever they went, Marat was known, and paid for little. He affected his customary boredom, but in fact enjoyed their pilgrimage, and augmented his pleasure by pressing Sand's nose, in passing, to the underbelly of the city—the human swamp, he called it, laughing savagely yet with curious compassion, discussing the people in theatrical tones, with meaningful tosses and shakes of his shaggy head, only to howl with amusement when Sand took him seriously, cursing crazily and coughing. And Sand walked with him in silence, absorbing everything he heard and saw, arranging and rearranging the puzzle of odd parts that littered his tired mind.

Nothing was done about their pursuer, whom Sand himself had noticed now. It was always a different person, trailing them skillfully, ceaselessly, remaining always on the opposite side of the street and far behind, and disappearing every little while to be replaced by another. Yet all shared a similarity which, though he could not define it, led him at last to the conviction that all of them were one. The difference was the newspaper, the missing tie, the turned-up collar, the turned-down hat, the eyeglasses, the overcoat worn like a cape or carried, the way of walking, and other devices, in endless combinations.

"He's good," Marat said one day. "Very good. If I hadn't trapped him that first evening, I might never have spotted the surveillance."

"What good has it done you? He's still there."

"Yes, he is. But I can get rid of him when the time comes."

They were eating *casse-croûte* in a café near the markets. A man paused opposite, in a doorway, face averted. Marat was discoursing on the prostitutes of Les Halles, their shocking old age and methods and the pathos of their noonday love with the butcher boys and peasant farmers in from the country with their produce, but at the sight of the man he went to the door. The man moved away down the street. Marat stared after him until he was out of sight. "He's damned good," he muttered, "but he doesn't know we know."

A huge whore garbed in fuchsia took the man's place in the doorway, in ambush like a spider in its cranny. And she was successful even before they left the café, preceding a covert man in rough country clothes into an anonymous entry near at hand.

"The people at play," Marat remarked. "Come, I will show you the people at work, since you seem so interested in God's image." He shouted good-by to the other customers, who shouted sourly in return, then glanced with suspicion at one another as if their shouts had somehow made them vulnerable. They had not said a word while Marat and Sand were present.

"Friendly, aren't they?" Marat grinned, outside. "But you must be polite to strangers here, for the worst cutthroats in Paris make this area their headquarters, and they are very particular about good manners, especially when they are drinking. Sometimes they go in pairs, to keep from feeling lonely, but they're a solitary lot, and very bitter about such bourgeois as yourself."

He glanced at Sand, who shrugged. "Alas," Marat intoned more loudly, "the criminal is only a poor unfortunate corrupted by bourgeois greed and turned against his noble fellows." Marat enunciated the jargon with relish, in a way that suggested that Sand was too naïve to share his joke and should

understand it literally. Sand, sensing this, could not bring himself to smile. He was dirty and tired and wanted more than
anything to bathe and sleep. But Marat kept him walking,
walking, night and day, and effectively prevented him from
doing either. "Come along, come along!" he would say every
time Sand dozed, "we have to go immediately!" But he never
said why they were going, and they never seemed to reach a
destination.

Sand could not think clearly any more, and, though he
suspected that Marat was wearing him down on purpose, he
wandered after him, too stubborn to complain.

They journeyed north on the Boulevard Sébastopol toward the Gare de l'Est, and by midafternoon had left the Faubourg Saint-Martin and were walking along the canal. The
area was oppressive, more resigned than poverty-stricken, as if
its natives had exchanged the aspirations of the very poor for
this bleak limbo beyond the slums—vast stretches of hard-
caked barren lots, and forlorn trees still standing here and
there, like weary sentinels.

Even Marat was subdued, picking his way along and pok-
ing at rubbish with a stick, as if searching the area for signs of
life. The canal itself was gray and still, and, unique among
municipal waters, held no attraction for children. Only, far
behind them, an old man made his way along, and once a
stoned dog darted out of a silent street and skirted past, its
nails clicking thinly on the concrete, too used to abuse even
to whine.

Sand spoke once all afternoon. "Are we going to Jacobi
now?" he said.

"To the abattoirs," Marat replied, "to see the people at
work." They were standing by a sullen pool where the Canal
Saint-Denis joined the Bassin de la Villette, and Marat pointed.
"Over there, to the right, is where the livestock are sold, and
there across the canal is where they are slaughtered. You will

find it interesting, I think." He turned and gazed back in the direction from which they had come. Sand, turning with him, saw the promenading old man stoop to retrieve something on the ground, then hobble off into a side street.

"He has had a long walk, our old man," Marat remarked.

They went west toward the Porte de la Villette. There, in one of the numerous noisy bistros opposite the abattoirs, Sand drank himself into a stupor. He did it on purpose, with an eye to the oblivion of sleep. Swaying by one hand from the zinc rail of the bar, he smiled softly to himself, overcome by the craftiness of his plan.

"I'm going to lie down," he informed Marat. "Right here on the floor, at the people's feet."

"Come on," Marat said. "I'll walk you around a little."

"You've walked me to hell and back," Sand said. "You've broken my spirit, that's all. You see before you—"

"Listen, my friend, if you want to see Jacobi you'd better do as I say."

"Listen, my friend, if you *want* me to see Jacobi you'd better take me there while I'm still stupid enough to go. And meanwhile I'm planning to lie down. I'm swooning dead away, in fact—"

Marat dragged him to a table by the wall and rolled him under it. Sand had a dim impression of shifting lights and the smell of sawdust and stale wine and a one-eyed, bearded demon who came and went and wrenched him from his sleep.

The dawn was drab and cold, and damp in the bone-baring way of Paris. Crossing with Marat to the abattoir gate, Sand shivered inside his turned-up collar and puffed at his cigarette without taking his hands from his pockets. He felt weak and filthy and sick—and uneasy, less at the prospect of what he was to see than about Marat's attitude in showing it to him, as if some dark secret of humankind was to be revealed.

They went first across the canal to the livestock shed, an enormous structure, open at the sides, which sheltered some thousands of animals. There were pigs, steers, sheep and goats, and tiny calves, each secured tightly by the head, wide-eyed and waiting; and among them their owners, thickset peasant farmers, shouted harshly over the din of their animals, often at nothing at all. Near the edges a prostitute, supported by a number of friends, was howling out a financial grievance at an unidentified member of the masculine herd, and other women vended coffee, and others waited in the empty trucks. A small urchin sat, rapt, among the calves, and a number of neighbor-hood dogs on skittish legs inspected the manure, the rich steam of which mingled with the sounds and smells in a jovial frontal attack on Sand's sensibilities. The spectacle was impressive, even exhilarating, and Marat himself could think of nothing cynical to say, for here life was too strong to bicker over or submit to politics.

And he only remarked, crossing the canal bridge to the slaughterhouses, "There is something heartening about that place; it gives off an odor of life's vitality and the people's essential strength." The idea that the Party could somehow take credit for this strength, which Sand inferred, was idly implied, out of long habit. "It gives also a feeling of human numbers," Marat continued, "if one thinks that by tomorrow night the great bulk of that meat will have disappeared down the city gullet and another huge herd will have replaced it. Especially when one realizes that the masses of the poor won't touch a bit." His wild face twisted in a scowl, and he seemed on the point of an oration, but thought better of it.

They passed a group of steers tied up outside a shed, and, entering, paused behind an executioner. Marat had an air of belonging wherever he went, despite his frenetic appearance, and the workers not only accepted his presence but promoted conversation. They seemed to feel that this man was one of them, and a leader besides, for remarks were invariably directed to him and not to Sand. Now the executioner turned from the steer which, straddling a fallen carcass, stood planted before him, and shouted to Marat, "So you've come to watch an expert do his work! Well, why not get us a bottle of wine, and show that you mean business, while you're at it!"

"Why don't you get on about your clumsy slaughter," Marat said "and stop stinking up the place with all your noise? You'll get a *coup de rouge* if you do it right, not otherwise."

The man approached them, smiling. "How about your friend?" he said, glancing at Sand. "Maybe he would like to buy a bottle? He doesn't have to go anywhere, I've got one right here, he can just pay me back my hundred francs!" Grinning broadly, he shoved a bloody palm in Sand's direction, and Sand, fumbling, found a bill.

Marat laughed and slapped the man on the shoulder. "Good for you," he said. "You've got a future ahead of you, my bloody friend."

The man retrieved a bottle from a corner and passed it around. The raw, cheap wine restored Sand's spirits, but before he could join the conversation the man had stepped away and picked up a sort of sledge hammer with a pointed head.

"I thought the law required pistols, *mon vieux!*" called Marat.

"Costs too damned much," the man shouted, and brought the hammer around his head in a swift neat arc, and down. The steer fell, kicking, to the crimson floor. Another man came forward with a heavy ax and proceeded to sever its head, the blows made more terrible by the crunch of the steel through bone. Then the stomach was sliced open and the entrails removed, and offal like green steaming moss wrung from the entrails into a pile by the wall.

"Very valuable material!" the executioner called. "Sorry I

can't spare you any of it!" He followed them outside, where Sand took a deep breath of air and drank heavily from the bottle. A woman selling cakes pushed her cart forward, and the man received one into his sticky hand without a trace of hesitation. "*A vous!*" he cried to Sand, hoisting the bottle, his mouth already full of cake. Sand managed a wave and followed Marat down the alley to the adjoining shed.

They witnessed the death of several steers and a number of screeching pigs, and Sand soon was hardened to the sight. He even felt a certain guilty exultation that he had not felt faint and weakened before Marat.

But his gusto wilted at the final shed, where the sheep met their end in groups of six. Unlike the cattle, the sheep ran frantically against their ropes and bleated in open panic, only to be seized up bodily and thrown onto a table on their backs. In this position they were pressed together like so many books on a shelf, their thin legs kicking in soiled clusters of twenty-four, and their six heads hanging, bleating, over the side of the table. Then a thin and sallow man passed along the row and slit their throats, and the blood shot out in sickening amounts, pouring away along a trough that split the center of the shed. The cluster of legs kicked on, ineffectual, and finally died.

"To hell with that," Sand said. He led Marat out the gate.

They crossed the street and had coffee in silence. Finally Marat said, "Well, did you enjoy it?"

"I'm glad we did it," Sand said.

"The people at work," Marat said. "It's rather ennobling, don't you think?"

"You make things too easy," Sand said. He nodded toward a sickly looking waiter with a dirty napkin over his arm, staring out the window. "That's the people at work too."

"Yes, there are the sheep as well. I'd almost forgotten." Marat frowned in irritation. "But Jacobi would tell you that cattle and sheep share a noble simplicity and are exploited the same way."

"In other words, he finds the people noble."

"Yes. Whereas I find them only less ignoble than their exploiters. Yet he dislikes people for the most part, and I like them." Marat smiled. "In Spain he used to abuse the priests unmercifully, for suppressing the people and telling them they were bad. As a child Jacobi was a Catholic himself, you see. He gave up the Faith, apparently, because he lost his job as choir leader. And he lost his job as choir leader because he humiliated the bishop's nephew for eating a chocolate during the *Cum Sancto Spiritu!*" Marat roared with laughter.

"Did he tell you that?" Sand said.

"Oh, he had more complicated reasons, of course, but he kept using the choir incident as an illustration of how the Church was rotten with special privilege, and political, like everything else. He didn't have much humor about it, poor Jacobi, and it's humor that gives a man perspective. Anyway, he forsook one dogma for another and could never quite discipline that angry mind of his to either. He's a born revolutionary, that's all. He'd die for the Party, but he'd die for his country too and never see the contradiction. A political idiot, but he made a fine soldier, I'll say that much." Marat raised his hand in an ironic salute to a phantasmal Jacobi, and with the other hand drew a finger across his throat.

"So the Party is this ruthless with him, after all these years, simply because he has a mind of his own."

"A mind of one's own, my friend, when indulged en masse, is a terribly inefficient thing. The Party is not being ruthless, but practical. It has a great deal to do"—here he gestured at a beggar who was singing in at them through the café door, over the shoulder of the waiter who barred his way—"and cannot afford to be sentimental over individuals."

"And you, Marat—don't you think for yourself?"

"Yes, But my mind is useful to the Party, the way Jacobi's heroism was useful."

"And when times change, and they decide that it's no longer useful?"

"Perhaps by that time I will be in a position to do the deciding. And if not—" He shrugged. "*Au revoir, cher Marat.* And this will be just, because I will have miscalculated the Party course, and could only blame myself."

"That's a chance you're willing to take, then?"

"I've already taken it," Marat said. "After a certain point of authority, one is held responsible, like Jacobi, for the people's protection against abuses. There is no turning back."

"For the people's protection?"

"Yes."

"You believe that sincerely."

"Do the religious believe in God?"

"Of course."

"Of course. One must believe in an ultimate purpose or accept all this as the sole reality." He nodded at the dirty window, which looked out upon a restaurant's side alley lined with garbage cans. From one of these cans two children were hoisting unidentifiable refuse into a burlap bag. "But do you see God out there? Or don't those children matter, so long as they die beneath the little fat white hands of a well-fed priest?"

"One need not accept men's churches to believe in a Force which we call God," Sand said. "Besides, that garbage may be for their cat." He felt cheated in the argument but unable to cope with it. He added, half to himself, "See, one of them is laughing."

"Oh, the people laugh, no doubt about it," Marat said, seizing his advantage. "It comes to them naturally, as it does to hyenas. They're cursed with hope. Before we're through, I'll show you where that hope gets them."

He went to the door, and after a moment Sand got to his feet and followed him.

Near the canal, that afternoon, a family of acrobats was staging an exhibition. The troupe was comprised of a man and a group of children, ostensibly his own, the smallest of whom, a fine-featured child of six or seven, alone had a costume. This was a doll-like golden frock of the sort worn by ballerinas and was too small for the little girl, and sadly soiled. She stood apart, however, smiling primly as the long, cold line of talented brothers and sisters were put through their paces, then danced forward and hopped onto her father's hands. He tossed her into the air, caught her about the knees, and, swinging her down and back through his legs, did a forward somersault at the end of which the child stood miraculously on her head upon his hands. At the hoarse request of the father, the passers-by gave sparingly of their applause. They showed no inclination to give anything else, however.

The father paused discreetly, then carefully, very carefully, lowered the child until, arching her back, she could touch her dainty heels to the ground on each side of his head. At a whisper from him she sniggered, winked upside down at the audience, and squatted over his face. To Sand's dismay, the father vented an oath, pushed her roughly aside, and in one way or another conveyed to the onlookers the idea that this elfin child, the golden apple of his eye, was all too mortal. Even worse, her indiscretion proved to be the climax of the act, a joke, and Sand realized that he alone in the crowd had not been aware of this, had not taken it in the spirit of fun in which it was meant. He stared stupidly amid the shouts of delighted laughter. And the little girl, having singled him out with unerring street instinct as the easiest mark, flounced forward with her father's hat. He backed away from her as Marat watched him. The people stopped smiling, intuitive and suspicious. Only at the last minute, when she stuck out her tongue, did he drop some coins into the battered hat, aware as he did so that he was giving much too much.

"How generous," Marat murmured. "But charity can hardly absolve you of responsibility."

"What are you after this time?" Sand snapped. "Responsibility for what?"

"For the people, for their poverty. If a girl is having your child, is it enough to contribute a diaper?"

Again Marat had him, and again Sand felt cheated, maneuvered into a position that gave him the choice of renouncing his own beliefs or his own behavior, when he would have preferred to believe that the two were aligned. And he knew he was no longer in a condition to resist this insidious man. As the days wore on he blundered after Marat from one stark revelation to another, unshaven, dirty, scarcely thinking, peering into the mirrors of public toilets for some sign of his past existence, past scale of values. He gave up asking Marat about Jacobi, drinking in the hopeless human lot that Marat delighted in demonstrating to him, and finally wondering to himself if the harsh cures of the Party were not, indeed, the sole solution.

For he was stunned by the vastness of this world he had never known, and the violence of it. His attention wandered more and more to sudden details, forsaking the static ugliness of factories and warehouses for the thin cafés, the fruit stands, tenement steps, and children in dark windows, and these in turn for the red eyes of an ancient woman seated in the gutter. Her dress was high on her blue legs, which stuck straight out like sticks into high tennis shoes, and the black grime on the old white of her thighs was the blurred design of penury.

"You!" she screeched at him. "You! Gave me thirty francs for coffee, eh? You and your filthy coffee will keep me awake all night!"

And Marat laughed.

From time to time Sand thought of breaking free. He wanted badly to go somewhere and think, not simply feel. He wondered too if the world he had known could ever be returned to, if he had not sunk down into the mud and stench of life without a trace, and if he would know the way back should Marat let him go.

12

Then one morning Sand ran away.

They had been drinking coffee in a *brasserie*. "I'm going to make a telephone call," Marat said. "You wait for me here."

Sand nodded, apathetic. He picked up Marat's newspaper and glanced at it without interest. There was a violent lead article against the government, which had staged a raid the night before on Party headquarters with the connivance of traitors within the Party itself. These, it said, would be exposed and punished by the full wrath of the people's justice.

Laying down the paper, he stared at the inner door through which Marat had disappeared. A man mopping up around the stacked metal tables slopped water on Sand's shoes, and, when Sand remonstrated, cursed him. Sand got up and went outside onto the sidewalk. His vague intent was to find some place to wash and sleep, and telephone Marat at the *brasserie* from there. But Marat had taken his billfold on the night he got drunk, to forestall any further initiative. He stood on the curb, intent on the dam of burlap sacking that channeled the gutter refuse into a drain. As long as he watched this eddy of dirty water he did not have to think.

But his fingers, searching still, found a subway ticket crumpled in a corner of his pocket.

Sand found himself trotting, almost running, toward the Métro. The sign on the entrance read PORTE-DES-LILAS. He clattered down the concrete stairs and glanced about for direction signs. Behind him there were other rapid footsteps echoing his own, but, turning, he saw only a flower-peddler with three bunches of withered violets. He ran on through the passageways and down another stairway, to the train platform, where he slipped through a closing automatic gate. Then he was hurtling along beneath the city, in a dream.

Climbing up out of the darkness at Odéon, he entered a different world. A weak sun shone, and a smiling girl in a pretty dress was buying hot chestnuts, and there was color in the air. He plunged across the boulevard against the traffic and into the rue de l'Ancienne Comédie and down the rue Saint-André to the rue des Grands Augustins. At Olivier's door he paused to catch his breath. But when he rang the bell, there was no response.

He rang again and again, and called, and finally pounded, without hope. Then the door burst open and a furious Lise appeared, flushed with sleep, disheveled. "Are you crazy?" she shouted. "I'm going to call the police, you filthy sot, what do you want here!" She recognized him and let him in.

He followed her through the apartment into her room, where she got back into bed. "All right, now, sit down," she said, patting the edge of the covers, and when he did so, she took his hand. "What is it, Bar-ney?" she whispered. "What has happened to you?"

And he shook his head in confusion, for nothing had happened; there was nothing he could explain even to himself, including his presence here. He started to speak, and stopped, and tried to smile.

Lise put her hand behind his head and drew it down beside her own on the pillow and stroked his cheek. He kissed her gratefully under the chin and closed his eyes. "Where's Olivier?" he muttered, though he did not care.

She laughed. "He isn't here," she murmured, "but for an unshaven, smelly tramp you leap quickly to conclusions, my dear Bar-ney." She wasn't in the least offended, but, on the contrary, quite coy; and although this was her way, Sand was encouraged to take her in his arms. The only warmth he had known in weeks was this sleepy form beside him, and he clung to it desperately and tried to kiss her.

"No," she whispered, "please don't, please." But her voice trembled, she was aroused despite herself, and he did not release her.

"It's not what you think, Lise," he muttered. "I just want to hold you for a minute." He was astonished by his words but could not help himself.

"No. I wanted to comfort you, you're clearly not yourself. I—you have me in a weak position, I'll admit. I am susceptible in the early mornings." She laughed, but her laughter was firm. "I don't want you to," she said. "That is to say, I won't let you." She sat up.

"Lise—"

"You're not yourself," she repeated, pushing at him gently. Neither had seen Olivier in the doorway.

"I didn't expect to find you here, my friend," said Olivier quietly. When Sand opened his eyes, Olivier smiled. "I think Lise is right, you are not yourself. If you will come into the other room, I'll give you a cup of coffee."

Sand got up slowly and followed him, too stunned to speak. He was not sure how badly he had behaved, but since there was no real explanation to be made he sat in silence over his coffee, shaking his head in agony. He could not look Olivier in the eye.

But Olivier observed him, humming "Mademoiselle de Paris" under his breath and conducting the song discreetly with his spoon. When Sand looked up at last, Olivier smiled and said, "Barney, my friend, you must try to see beyond what you are seeing these days, or it will blind you, as they wish. You must be careful. Of course I am only guessing, I—"

"What do you mean? Olivier, I'm very sorry."

"No, listen to me. I should not say this to you, and you must not tell Gleize or Marat that I've said it. I am not supposed to know as much as I have guessed. But why do you go on with it, whatever it is? You must consider the situation. You are in trouble, Barney. Look at you, they are doing something to you!"

"Maybe I've given up," Sand said. "Maybe that's why I'm here. I must explain to you about Lise. I—I'm confused; I need sleep or something. I need to talk to somebody."

Olivier threw his hands into the air, then slapped them down upon his knees. "Of course! That doesn't matter! You must give up what you are doing, that's all. Gleize is coming here now to take you back. But you must not be a fool. You are not dealing with reasonable people any more, they don't think the way you do!"

"No!" Sand said, standing up. "I apologize for trying to excuse myself, Olivier. There is no excuse, none at all!" He was seized with revulsion for himself. Something was giving way in him, he wanted badly to cry, and this realization enraged him further.

Then Rudi Gleize slipped into the room, his pale face moist with perspiration. "Thank you for telephoning," he said to Olivier, then darted at Sand and seized him by the wrist. "Have you gone mad!" he grated. "Do you want to spoil everything? Come along!"

Sand knocked Rudi Gleize away from him. "There's something I have to say to Olivier before I go."

Olivier shook his head. "No, there isn't," he said sadly. He was stirring his cold coffee as Sand preceded Rudi through the door.

On the stairwell three bunches of withered violets recalled the flower-peddler at the Porte-des-Lilas. "You're forgetting your violets," he said to Rudi, picking them up.

Rudi glared at him. "What is it?" he complained. "What are you up to now? Come along. Where did you leave Marat?"

Descending the stairs, Sand held the violets in his hand. Who, then? he thought. Olivier? But what did it matter, what did anything matter? He hurled the violets into the gutter.

Rudi escorted Sand as far as the Porte-des-Lilas. "Go back to that *brasserie,*" he said. "I'll be watching from the Métro entrance." They were ascending the stairs to the street.

Sand stopped. "You've been having me followed, haven't you?"

"I am keeping an eye on you," Rudi admitted after a moment's hesitation. "You are a friend, and I would hate to see you get into trouble."

"What sort of trouble?"

"There won't be any trouble," Rudi said, "no trouble at all. Just do as Marat tells you — everything he tells you—and there won't be any trouble. No, why do you look at me that way? I tell you, I am your friend, I am keeping an eye on you just in case!" he exclaimed, producing a ghastly smile. "But you must not spoil all my efforts by being foolish! I sometimes wonder why I take so much trouble for you!"

"No doubt you find virtue its own reward," Sand said. "You miserable bastard."

He took no further notice of Rudi Gleize, turning his back on the man and proceeding slowly along the sidewalk. Why have I come back, he wondered, why didn't I keep running? He had been defeated by his search, and dirtied, and he wanted to believe he could blame on its effects his betrayal of Olivier.

Olivier is your friend, he thought. Don't those things matter any more? He flushed anew with self-contempt, and his step quickened masochistically in the direction of Marat's café.

He knew he was afraid of Marat, afraid of this man's plans for him, afraid of the relentless effort to disgust him with humanity and thus prove to them both that Sand, corrupted by the background on which Marat had turned his back, could not stomach human degradation, much less accept responsibility for it. He was afraid of all this, but he understood Marat's compulsion. He did not yet understand why Marat was degrading him as well.

Entering the café, he gritted his teeth in a last surge of resolve, so fiercely that the waiter drew back against the bar. At the latter's sulky sneer, Sand laughed in exasperation. To me you are the people, he said silently to the man, I wonder why you sulk, but Marat—Marat is too busy talking about you even to notice you.

Marat sat at a table in the rear, watching the door. "So you ran away, did you?" he said, clenching Sand's upper arm in his huge fist. "I should have known your sort could not be trusted!"

"What made you so sure I'd come back at all?" Sand asked.

"The same reason that made me think you wouldn't go away—you're too stubborn to give up after coming so far."

"I'm too stupid, isn't that what you mean?"

"You were stupid to leave! I have half a mind to drop the whole affair!"

"You won't, though," Sand said. "You need me more than I need you." He had not intended this as a bluff, but Marat released his arm and changed his approach.

"And on top of everything else, he brings this creature

Gleize back with him!" Rolling his good eye in frustration, he
smashed his fist down on the table, but the other customers
of this listless neighborhood paid no attention. "Don't deny
it!" He pushed his volatile face at Sand. "I was keeping watch
from the window."

"Everybody seems to be keeping watch," Sand said, "except for me." He took a piece of sugar from the saucer and
broke it in half. "And everybody is trying to outsmart everybody else, except for me." He gazed at Marat. "Can you explain that?"

"You're subtle, my friend," Marat said, gauging him, "but
it's too late to talk nonsense now. You admit Gleize is trailing
us."

"He says he is keeping an eye on me," Sand said, and
grinned a loose, disembodied grin, as if he were drunk. "He
says he is my friend."

"And it hadn't occurred to you, I suppose, that locating
Jacobi's whereabouts might also be of interest to him?"

"Yes, I knew that. But only because he told me so before
we started. I didn't connect him with the man who follows us,
though. Our man is taller than Rudi Gleize, you see. You
should have noticed that, Marat; you're the crafty type, not
me." Sand tried to stop smiling but could not. He felt irresponsible and giddy. "No, I'm not subtle, as you put it. You
only think so because you don't understand how my mind
works. It doesn't work like yours. I'm simple-minded, or something. Simple-hearted. I'm so simple-hearted that I go on hoping to see Jacobi even though it's become quite clear that
you've got some sort of nasty surprise in store for me, that I
may even be in danger. And do you know why I go on, Marat?
Do you know why?"

"You say you're a journalist. You'll have quite a story."

"You don't believe I'm a journalist?"

"Of course, of course. Get on with it, whatever it is."

"All right. No, the story was only the original impetus, the sop to practicality. I think I was searching for something, perhaps the something-to-believe-in you mentioned a few days ago. Or was it weeks? But after what you've shown me, Marat, I find it hard to have faith in anything at all except myself—except what I feel, what I think, what I know. And if I give up the search I won't even be able to have faith in *that*. Do you understand me?"

"I don't believe you."

"No, I suppose you don't. It's not really believable, is it?" Sand started to laugh. Through the mist in his eyes he could see Marat studying him, perplexed at first, then slowly triumphant, but he didn't care. He didn't care any longer about anything.

Marat got up and, coming around behind Sand, picked him up in his chair and turned him around and set him down again, hard, so that he was planted, laughing still, before a mirror on the wall.

"Take a good look," Marat said. "Do you believe in that?"

The poor wretch in the mirror laughed at Sand, though his eyes were wet with tears, and, blinking, Sand caught his breath and the laughter stopped. Marat's fingers, pressed into his shoulders, held him face to face with that thin, stubbled image, the gaunt neck in the filthy collar, the tie like a hanging shred of rope, the eyes like wounds.

"I don't know," he said. "I think so."

"The teeth—" Marat said, "notice the teeth, for they are the only part of the skeleton that shows, and should remind you of it. There is a skull behind those eyes, a death's head. One is alive or one is dead, but one is never more than what you see before you."

"Perhaps I see more than you are able to." Sand's voice was monotone.

"We're wasting time," Marat said. "We have to go. Tomorrow you're to see Jacobi, but while there's still light I will show you what all your hope will come to."

Following Marat to the door, Sand passed the mirrors on the walls. He wondered if he saw an individual in change, or only images of a man named Barney Sand, an animal, Homo sapiens, a life.

13

"Death!" Marat shouted, striding through the cemetery like some fiendish guide, his black raincoat blowing out behind him. "Look at it all, as far as the eye can see—isn't it stupefying! The speechless ones!" He waved his great arms up and down as if summoning these silenced voices to rise in a chorus of protest. An old groundskeeper raking leaves along the path shook his head disapprovingly as Marat and Sand approached.

And Marat said to the old man, "It won't be long now, eh, Grandpère? Next year's dead leaves, perhaps, will include your funeral flowers!"

Curiously, the old man smiled. "Until then, I'm a better man than you, my noisy friend," he said, and Marat laughed.

"Good for you!" he said. "And you look like a tough old vulture, you'll probably bury us all!"

"Yes," the old man said, "and loot your graves, besides. But meanwhile I feel the need of a glass of wine. Perhaps, *chers messieurs*, we could find a café together—"

"No, thanks very much, you are too kind." Marat bowed ceremoniously, smiling. "But we have business here."

The old man shook hands and nodded good-by in silence.

They went walking down the ordered rows, over the bones

of centuries. There was an air of endless autumn about the cemetery, with its great trees and creeping moss and masses of pale stone, and the clatter of life from beyond its walls rang thin, like a tin toy trumpet. Among the trees there stood a makeshift fencing, sagging and rotten black with rain, and the surrounding earth was soft with leaves and a curious white clay. Marat went around behind the fence and pointed down into the enormous trench that it hid from the formal cemetery. "Here we have humility even after death," he murmured, smiling unpleasantly, "the final resting place of the poor." And, as Sand peered down in horror, Marat said pompously, "Here lies humanity."

The pit was roughly fifteen feet in depth, and five-by-fifteen yards in area. The near end held only scattered bones submerged in a pool of rain water, but extending outward from the far end was a vast amorphous heap of human skeletons, stacked up like so much cord wood. A number of skulls had rolled down from the summit and lay in the edge of the water, and the bones still bore the vestiges of flesh, in odd white weightless clusters. These nearer remains, fresh from the single graves, were tinged with cemetery moss, but the older ones, disappearing back beneath the earth at the closed end of the trench, were bare and sour yellow.

Sand, seeing the white clay clinging to his shoes, realized that the pit was endless, extending beneath the soil far back among the old trees of this silent place. It was the quiet, the peaceful descent of leaves into the pit, that overcame him, not with revulsion, for there was no odor but the autumn, not even with pity, for the remains had little character, hardly more than the leaves and fallen twigs. There came instead a profound sadness, a regret, and whether it stemmed from this heaped-up mute indignity or the perspective it gave him on the meaning of his quest he was unable to determine, then or later. And he found himself too moved to break the silence.

But Marat, watching, misinterpreted and said, "You must not be horrified. They have had their turns in separate boxes, but room had to be made for others. There are so many others." He grimaced wryly, waving his hand at the vast reaches of the cemetery and the crowded rooftops beyond the wall.

"Why did you bring me here?" Sand spoke for the first time.

"I've already told you. I wanted to prove my point. This is the result of all man's hope, including yours." Marat kicked a small bone from the clay at the edge of the pit and sent it skittering down among the broken skeletons. "*Requiescat in pace*," he said.

"And why do you want to prove this to me? What can it matter to you what I think?"

"You seem to have a sense of responsibility about the people, despite your past. The Party would be willing to forget the past, if you chose to make yourself useful." He cocked his good eye at Sand.

"And if I don't cooperate?"

Marat caught a falling sycamore leaf and spun its stem between thumb and forefinger. "You won't have much choice. But cooperation will make things much simpler for everybody, especially if you believe you are doing right."

"In acting against Jacobi? Is that what you want of me?"

"In acting for the Party, for the people."

"What's happened to him doesn't affect you, then, even though you were friends."

"I can't permit myself to be affected, by friendship or anything else—even this." He pointed at the paupers' bones. "I haven't time."

"No, you haven't time," Sand said, speaking slowly at first, his voice rising, quickening, "even to be honest. To get what you want you've worn down my resistance, and you've shown me only the underside of humankind, the animal, the weak,

the lost, and now the dead. The irretrievable, in other words."
He gestured at the green and yellow bones, the faceless skulls.
"But I feel pity still, while you, *you haven't time* for pity, you
regard people clinically, like domestic animals, and you manip-
ulate them politically, like tin soldiers, isn't that true, Marat?
And isn't it true of the Party itself—that it hasn't time for
pity, as you say?"

Marat stood silent, watching Sand. "Yes, it's true," he said
some seconds later. "Because our methods are scientific, and
science is a scalpel, not a sentimental tear. The rot must be
cut away, however ruthlessly. It can't be cured by pity. We
leave the individual for you to pray over, but humanity is ours,
and we mean to do the job.

"Of course," he added, "the political factor is unavoidable,
since we are bound to meet resistance on many frontiers, and
sometimes from the people themselves. To a certain extent
they resemble their governments in being selfish, and terrified
of change. Then harsh methods become necessary, and I don't
deny that these have been used and will be used again. But
what are the few who are sacrificed today compared to the
legions who will benefit tomorrow? Most human beings have
everything to gain by a social revolution, whatever they may
think of the Party. What do your precious liberties mean to
the great starving hordes in Asia and Africa? Yet your society
still propagates the falsehood that they cannot hope for more
in life than religion and the status quo, plus charity and cheap
reforms when religion no longer sustains them. Whereas we
are working with a truth—the world is in need of drastic
change—and therefore the political factor is beneficial to us
in the long run. You people cannot face that truth, you attack
the Party for unrest that was inevitable, and so you must go
on fighting, and losing, what Jacobi used to call the Great
Twentieth-Century War."

"You're so very sure you're right, aren't you?" Sand said,

inept against this logic which, though bulwarked by basic right, lost its ring of truth through the deft fingers playing on the surface of the bell.

"Perhaps. But so are you." Marat laughed, delighted with himself.

They turned abruptly at a cough behind them, and Marat's laughter faded, chastened, in the stillness. A man was leaning on the corner of the fencing, face half averted, watching them from the corners of his eyes. His head nodded up and down, up and down, and his shiny rotten mouth hung open in a snarl. He was carrying a stick with a pointed end, of the sort used to pick up trash and wastepaper in public places, and a burlap bag over his ragged shoulder.

"Eh?" he said. "You find something amusing here, messieurs?" The snarl shifted momentarily into something like a smile, but there was no true alteration in his expression. "You are laughing at the poor, perhaps, messieurs"—and he raised his stick and pointed at the bone pile—"and yet you have no rights here. You should leave us in peace, messieurs, we are only poor unfortunates, we have done nothing to harm you, messieurs—"

"What do you want?" Marat demanded.

"No, monsieur, it is we who ask you what *you* want. A skull, perhaps? You are a medical student, monsieur, are you not? Perhaps you do not wish to spend your money on a skull, and thought to steal one here, is that it? Oh, there are many like you, I myself have seen them, monsieur, I keep a careful watch here, you know."

The man came a little closer. Although not old, he hobbled weakly, leaning on the trash stick for support. His face was gaunt and sick, his garments filthy, and though he wore no beard, he was long unshaven. Beneath the stubble the skin was swollen red, and his odor was the odor of stale wine. The decay and drunkenness were long since ingrained in him, for even his eyelids were raw and sagging and his skin a network of veins.

"Medical students, eh? I keep a careful watch, messieurs." He winked at them, then scowled.

"I'm going, Marat," Sand said, starting away.

"No," Marat snapped. "It is not we who are in the wrong. This is the other kind I mentioned, the demented kind." And he said to the man, "Then it is you who sells the skulls, monsieur—you make a living at it, isn't that it?"

The man crouched back, suspicious, and pointed his stick at them. "Eh? It is you who are the thieves, messieurs, I have seen many like you, you have come to disturb the poor in their final rest, you think they have no rights because you see them dumped in here like garbage to make way for the rich! Eh? The rich!" The man cursed vilely, spitting onto his chin. "But I am here to protect them, and it is you who have no rights here. You have only come to steal their skulls, and sell them, no doubt, to others like yourselves!" He nodded wisely, to indicate his knowledge of the ways of the world, but a terrible greed was now apparent in his face, and his hands worked furiously on his stick. "But I am here to protect these poor bones, messieurs, and you must deal with me—another poor man like these others, messieurs, but not a thief, messieurs, not a heartless thief!" At this point, still scowling horribly, the man burst into tears.

"Since we are to deal with you," Marat said to him, "please name your price. Do you sell by the dozen, or five at a time?" He was walking slowly toward the retreating figure, which felt its way backward around the corner of the fencing, breathing hoarsely and coughing, the stick still pointed at Marat.

"Do not annoy us with your self-justifications, monsieur," Marat was saying. "Come, you are a businessman, I can see it in your face! Simply name your price and have done with it!"

"I am not like yourselves!" the man screeched. "I am not a thief! You will only sell these bones for a higher price, out in the street! And I, a poor sick man, will have to go to all the trouble of climbing down into the trench, and risk losing my position of guardian in the bargain, only to let you make a profit behind my back! No, I am not like yourselves, messieurs, though you take me for a fool. I am an honorable man!"

"Then we will simply take what we wish without your help," said Marat, starting back toward the pit.

Immediately the man broke down. "Thieves! Thieves!" he screamed, hobbling forward. "You have no right; it is up to me! You are only trying to threaten a poor man, messieurs, to cheat me of my price!"

Marat whirled upon Sand, throwing his arms out in a violent gesture, then stamped furiously around the pit. "Ha!" he shouted. "You see, he has his price, this noble creature!" He shook both fists in the air, his great wild face contorted in rage, in exaltation and insane glee. Then he charged the cringing man and shook him by the shoulders as a dog shakes a rat and hurled him violently against the fencing, as if to frame him there for the world's inspection.

"Look at him!" Marat shouted. "Regard, *messieurs-dames*, this proud specimen of mid-century man, this tribute to civilization, this citizen of Western democracy, this animal! Do you note a paradox, *messieurs-dames*, does it not strike you that something is amiss in our modern world?" Marat's voice broke and fell away in the autumn silence like an echo.

"Marat," Sand said, and Marat turned to him. His face was working in spasms of emotion, and once again everything was there, the rage and glee, the love and hate, as if in his strange features the feelings of all humankind had mixed and were building toward some shattering burst of vain expression. It was impossible to guess what Marat might do next, for there was every action in that face, and for a moment Sand recalled what Marat had once said. I *am the people! Look at me, Sand, and remember!* And Sand remembered.

But now he could bear the scene no longer, and he moved away across the white clay earth, abandoning Marat to his prey, who, in great alarm at Sand's departure, had scrambled, ratlike, down into the pit and was squeaking out his prices. On the path Sand turned and, glancing back, saw Marat haul the other from his hole and give him money. He leaned on an iron rail, exhausted.

"All right," Sand said when Marat came. "I have to agree with you."

"That the Party is right?"

"No. That it is working with a truth. I mean, that the world is in need of change."

"So you'll cooperate?"

"I don't know," Sand said. "I'm choosing between wrongs."

They went on down the narrow path between the graves. Beyond the wall and the jaundiced rooftops a gray wind shifted the November sky and stirred the darkness of late afternoon. This was the hour of solitude, Sand thought, of ultimate reality. Beneath his weary feet the path seemed endless, stretching away forever between life and death.

14

Sand and Marat, leaving the cemetery, went south to the Place de la Nation, and from there to Bastille, where they had their supper in a restaurant. Marat obtained an evening paper, which headlined further details of the government raid on Party headquarters. He was restless, and over coffee said to Sand, "It's time to get rid of our shadow."

Sand did not trouble to answer. He was brooding about the meeting with Jacobi and weighing his own attitudes. Foremost among these was a mighty impulse to be clean, severe, to cut away at filth, to strike out at the greed for wealth and power that diseased the world. How simple that would be, he thought—to know you were right, to act without having to think! How very simple, were he certain of the Party's sincerity and of his own, were he only unaware of what might happen to him should he decide against the Party now. For he knew he was afraid.

He studied the man across the table, the man within whose power he had placed himself. Once, as a boy, he had seen a mouse trapped in an eddy of a stream, struggling to escape the vortex but succeeding only in circling disaster, round and round and round, and weakening.

"No, I have a better idea," Marat was saying slowly, as if

outlining the plan to himself. "He is very skillful, whoever he is, and we would have trouble eluding him. Then, if we do try to elude him, it is more than likely that Gleize will put several people on the job, too many to take care of at the last minute. But one man can be taken care of, you see, and so we will let him follow us until tomorrow morning. And to make sure he doesn't call for assistance in the meanwhile we will spend the night where he can keep an eye on us most easily." Marat smiled in satisfaction. "So—" He rapped the table with his forefinger. "I want you to sit right there for a moment," he said.

Sand watched him rise and shoulder his way to the telephone at the end of the counter. It occurred to him to run, yet he did not. The flight to Olivier and Lise had exhausted the last of his initiative, and Marat seemed to sense this, for he was indulgent with Sand and, with victory in his hand, almost affectionate.

They left the restaurant and walked southwest toward the river, coming out at last at one end of the bridge. Marat strolled to the middle of the bridge and there turned and leaned back against the parapet, looking casually in the direction from which they had come. After a moment he muttered to Sand, "You see, he's still with us. There, going into that *tabac* on the corner."

Sand did not look around, but instead leaned forward over the wall and stared into the dark swirl of the Seine, then down the river toward the Ile Saint-Louis. "It's quiet tonight," he said after a while.

"The view from the bridges is the finest in the city," Marat answered. "It shows Paris at its best—that is to say, at its most artificial and romantic." He gestured with grandiose irony at the night silhouettes in the distance. "But *under* the bridges one finds another Paris, as typical as the other in its way." He pushed himself up and started off again toward the other end,

where they descended the concrete steps to the river quai and
sat down on a bench against the high white wall.

"He can't miss us here," Marat said. After a time he rose
again and led Sand under the head of the bridge. "This is the
perfect place to spend the night," he explained with satisfaction. "He can pin us down with no trouble at all, for there is
no escape. Besides"—and he nodded into the shadows—"we
will have the company of charming companions."

Sand looked again at what he had taken to be an amorphous pile of refuse and made out here and there a stringy
head, a crusted shoe. The damp stone and concrete reeked of
stale urine, and it was clear from a small charred pile of stones,
a sort of pathetic hearth, that a number of people made this
shelter their home.

"What more could one ask?" Marat was saying. "A lovely
view, a picnic, clear nights *al fresco* on the river among one's
charming friends—"

"Go away," a hoarse voice croaked, "and leave a poor man
in peace. You're setting up an echo here, with all your nonsense!"

"Shut up, old imbecile-drunkard-sot," Marat said affably,
"or I'll toss the lot of you into the river."

"Good idea," another voice said. "Might clean him up a
little. You have a little wine, dear friend?"

"No, and no money either, in case you have any ideas."
Marat sat down a little apart from them, against the wall. "You
must keep goats here, from the smell," he said.

"Ah well," a third voice said, "one can't have everything
in life, they say. And besides, the least you could do is lie over
here and help us get a little warmth." The voice was plaintive,
injured, and the other voices muttered assent. "He thinks he
is too good for us," one whined, and broke into a racking
cough.

Marat laughed. "It's not that, my friends, it's because I'm

ashamed of my dirty fingernails, and would risk infecting you
with my runny nose."

But later in the night, with evident distaste, Marat shoved
away an old man who fumbled near him for a place to lay his
head. The man lit a match and peered at Marat in alarm, and
Sand, half dozing, had a glimpse of a green ring of charity
soup around the white-whiskered mouth and the sharp, small
chin of age. He remembered the figure with the fallen pigeon,
beneath the Pont du Carrousel. Then the match flickered, and
the image was gone.

They left the bridge early in the morning and walked
through the cold gray mist along the river edge. Sand was stiff
with a chill that had penetrated to the deepest areas of his
body. He stumbled after Marat, miserable, unthinking, and did
not respond when Marat said, "Do you see him? He is trailing
us from above, along the bookstalls."

Sand saw an elderly rakish man moving along above and
behind them, saluting the booksellers with a cane and pausing
now and again to inspect a volume or an ancient print. Arching his back, he would hold the book away from him at arm's
length, cane tucked up under his arm, and clear his throat
angrily in apparent mystification about the character of the
item. The pose, exaggerated and comic, brought laughter from
his audience, and Sand recognized it at once. The man was
Olivier.

The identity troubled him, but only for a moment. Olivier
had to be warned away. As they moved along the quai Sand
put his hand behind him and waved Olivier back. The gesture
felt clumsy and ineffectual, and it did not work, for, looking
up a minute later, he saw that Olivier still followed, whistling
in a breezy manner a song about two snails.

"Stop looking at him," Marat snapped. "You'll scare him
off."

And Sand cursed Olivier for a fool. Look at him, he

thought, marching into an ambush whistling, and overplaying his part to get attention for himself.

They mounted to the street once more and entered a café. "You'll need a camera," Marat said, "to corroborate your interview."

Sand gazed at him.

"Otherwise who will believe you?" Marat said.

Sand nodded vaguely. "All right," he said. "A camera might be a good idea." They had a second coffee, waiting in silence until the shops had opened, when they obtained for Sand a small cheap camera and film. Then they went on again, up the Left Bank in the direction of Montparnasse.

In a street near Notre-Dame-des-Champs they entered a tiny bar. The sign in its window said that the place was closed. The chairs were stacked upon the tables, and the barman who let them in was alone in the place. He returned behind the counter but made no attempt to serve them. Instead he watched the door. Marat lit a cigarette, and Sand stood, feeling foolish, clutching the package with the camera in it.

Within minutes a bespectacled drunk reeled past the window, glaring inside as he passed. Marat nodded to the barman, who went to the window and rapped on it. Two men in a doorway across the street moved rapidly in the direction taken by the drunk, and after a moment returned with him to the bar. Protesting loudly in a strange falsetto voice, he was pushed up against the counter next to Marat.

"*Zut! Il y a des limites, quand même!*" he squeaked, rearranging his jacket. "A man can't even take the air any more without being attacked in broad daylight! It is a disgrace to the nation to have such trash as yourselves loose in the streets!"

They watched him in silence.

"Well, messieurs? What is it you want with me? Perhaps one of you is optimistic about my finances? Oh, I am no child, messieurs, I am well acquainted with the ways of the world, dirty place that it is, and crawling with such filth as yourselves—"

"That's enough," Marat told him. "I want to know why you are following us."

"Following you? On the contrary, it is you who follow me, and seize me, yes, and drag me like a sheep into this den!"

"Who are you working for?" Marat asked. "I advise you to answer quickly, my friend."

"Working for? You are speaking to a gentleman, *cher monsieur*, I do not need gainful employ. I am of the leisure classes." He brushed a little at his lapels and winked at one of the men who had brought him to the bar. This man winked back, sarcastically, and returned his gaze to Marat, who leaned forward and tweaked the drunk's heavy nose.

"Coward!" the drunk screamed. "Pig!"

The actor's paste came away in Marat's fingers. Then Marat knocked the man's cap from his head, and with it the heavy spectacles.

"I thought so!" Marat shouted with laughter. "So it was you, Olivier, all the time!"

Olivier grinned ruefully, rubbing his nose. "I'll have a cognac, please," he said to the barman, "since you gentlemen insist on making a party of it." He winked at Sand, then glanced apprehensively at Marat.

But the latter was laughing still, a personal laugh flecked with anger. "Cognac it is," he said. "He deserves it!" He slapped Olivier on the shoulder, a little too roughly. "And you were the old gentleman on the quai this morning too, eh, my friend?"

In answer, Olivier removed his seedy jacket and turned it inside out. The inside, complete with pockets and lapels, was of different material, and in good repair; and from its pockets Olivier, with the mannered grace of a magician, drew forth a pince-nez, a tiny make-up kit, a toupee, a folding opera hat, and a telescoping cane.

"The old gentleman on the quai," he murmured, eyebrows elevated in astonishment, "entered a *pissoir*, never to be seen again. But wait"—and now his eyes assumed a conspiratorial gleam, and he held up his finger for their attention—"from this very same *pissoir*, messieurs, there emerged some moments later an entirely different individual, a notorious drunkard, a swinish good-for-nothing—" He downed his cognac and offered a bleary smile. "Well, messieurs, many thanks," he said in the falsetto voice once again. "I am delighted to learn that chivalry is not yet dead in La Belle France, and that drunks will not go thirsty. Now, if you will excuse me—" But he made no move to depart.

Marat watched him. "Who are you working for?" he asked, his expression so cold that the laughter in the room hung frozen in the air.

"I was simply amusing myself," Olivier said. "You know how I am, I like to try out my disguises, I am thinking of giving up sculpture for the *cirque*, I—"

"That's enough," Marat told him. "You'd better tell us."

"Oh, what I've said is true enough," Olivier said quite sincerely. "I am a fool at heart, as everybody knows. And then, I wanted to keep an eye on our good friend"—he nodded at Sand—"to make sure he got into no serious trouble, you know."

"And who else is interested besides yourself?"

"Why, Lise, of course; she is very fond of him."

"Lise has a way of being fond of other men, doesn't she, Olivier? I remember another occasion, on the Spanish border—"

Olivier flushed. "That's not kind of you," he said to Marat. Marat flushed himself. "I'm not a kind person, my friend; I haven't time." But he leaned forward and placed his hand gently on Olivier's shoulder. "You'd better tell us," he said. "I'd rather not do anything unpleasant."

"All right," Olivier said. "What difference does it make? Monsieur Gleize, too, is a good friend to Sand, and asked me to keep an eye on him, in case he got into trouble."

"Why did you hesitate to tell us? Did it occur to you that Monsieur Gleize might have a more practical reason?"

"You already have your opinion about it, Marat. What I say won't do much to change it."

"No, it won't." Marat watched Olivier sit down slowly on a chair, then took the barman and the other two aside.

Sand moved toward Olivier, who, clutching like toys the knickknacks of his costume, presented a sorry spectacle. His long neck was bent and mute in the classic sadness of the clown, and his hands were crossed upon his chest in a way that was genuine in the same way it was false; for the pose, though artificial, was spontaneous. Then, glancing up at Sand, he smiled.

"I tried to warn you," Sand whispered. "I waved you back."

"I know. I thought you would sprain your wrist."

"Then you knew we'd discovered you?"

Olivier nodded. "Of course," he murmured. "Since the night you left the bookstore, and Marat set that trap for me." He observed Sand's bewilderment with childish pleasure. "Gleize was prepared for that. Gleize knew the Party was used to surveillance, that it was only a matter of time before I was noticed. And when Marat did nothing about it right away, he guessed immediately what Marat had in mind, you see."

"Well, Marat outsmarted him. Here you are."

Olivier shook his head. "No," he said. "Marat has always had a tendency to outsmart himself. He did it last night by encouraging surveillance. I knew things were about to happen, and telephoned Gleize from the *tabac*. Gleize is still one step ahead of him." Olivier shrugged, with an expression of distaste, and changed the subject. "You didn't take my advice, Barney, and now it's too late."

"I could still give it up—"

"It's too late," Olivier repeated, nodding toward the others. "You must cooperate with Marat now, you have no choice."

"No," Sand said. "I suppose I don't."

"Ask him to leave Lise alone, please, Barney," Olivier blurted suddenly, upset. "Poor Lise has nothing to do with this."

"He won't do anything, Olivier, I'll tell him," Sand said. Marat had stopped talking to his men and was watching them. "And Olivier about Lise the other day—you've been a good friend to me, I—"

Marat came toward them, and Olivier took Sand's hand. "Speak to Marat about Lise and you'll be just as good a friend to me," he said.

Marat led Sand to the door. Olivier watched them go, and gave a slight wave of the hand when Sand glanced through the window. One man stood by the chair, and the other was gesturing to the barman.

"Poor Olivier," Marat said. "They'll probably rough him up a little."

"Why? What's the sense in it?"

"People always assume that Olivier is naïve, even a little stupid. It is very useful to him. But he has to be discouraged from betraying the Party."

"He's not betraying it, he's not even in it. He resigned."

"The Party does not accept resignations," Marat said, and grinned malevolently. "And even an opponent, acting against it, is considered to be betraying it. You'd be surprised how simple these principles make things."

Sand stopped short on the sidewalk. "At least give me your word not to trouble Lise," he said.

"You're not in a position to make demands."

"I know," Sand said. "I'm asking it of Marat, not the Party."

They walked on a little way. "All right," Marat said. "You trust my word, then?"

"Shouldn't I?"

"Well, since you do already, you inspire me to keep it." Marat gave Sand his hand, then hailed a passing taxi. He leaned into the driver's window and whispered an address.

In the taxi, he seized Sand by the scruff of the neck and forced his head forward against the back of the front seat. "You're not feeling well," he muttered. "Keep your eyes on the floor until we get there." After a moment he removed his hand.

Sand blinked at the filthy cigarette butts broken in the grime and the dull toes of his own weathered shoes. He felt degraded, beaten, in this bent position, and his eyes misted over with rage at Marat's action. He said quietly, intensely, "You didn't have to do that, did you? You didn't have to do so much of what you've done. And it's because you're unsure of yourself, and ashamed of your own origins, that you've tried so hard to punish me for mine, isn't that it? You're afraid."

"Afraid?" Marat's jeering laugh was high, exaggerated. "You sound a little nervous, Sand, yourself."

Sand's forehead jarred upon the metal, and he placed his hand beneath it. The position reminded him of church and that forward squat of token prayer which, keeping him from kneeling, had made him feel less insincere about his presence there each Christmas. Perhaps I should pray now, he thought. He cursed instead.

"All right," Marat said. The taxi slowed.

Sand leaned back against the seat and tried to collect himself. Concentrate, he told himself, you've got to concentrate.

When the taxi halted, Marat took Sand by the elbow and led him into a building.

"Just go to the top floor," he said, "and tell the guard your name. He'll take you to Jacobi." Marat looked at his watch. "I'll give you forty minutes for your interview."

"And then?"

"And then I see no reason why you shouldn't leave."

"I thought you expected me to cooperate in some way."

"You're cooperating nicely." Marat smiled. "Just leave everything to me."

"I'm not going up there," Sand said.

"Yes, you are," Marat told him, putting his right hand into his pocket. "The gentleman is expecting you."

Sand mounted the stairs, out of breath from the beating of his heart. He wondered if he would have fled even had Marat let him. It was like walking to the sea on a chilly day for the last swim of the year and forcing oneself into the agony of cold water. He had gone too far on principle to turn back in common sense.

At the landing he looked back down and saw Marat's white face in the dim hallway, like something lost on the bottom of a pool. Then the guard came down the stairs and gave Sand a mock salute. "All right, Marat?" he called.

"That's him," Marat said. "The eminent American journalist, Monsieur Sand."

Sand preceded the guard up the stairs. He waited while the man turned a key in the lock. Then he entered Jacobi's room, and the door closed behind him.

15

Jacobi sat on a small hard chair in the center of the room. He sat with his hands clenched, fingers inward on his knees, the way an old man sits who has walked a long way uphill, as if he wanted to go on but could not get his breath. He wore a black suit and a white shirt and a tie, and he did not rise when Sand entered.

"I was expecting you," he said, expressionless. His hair was still dark, and his swart, clean-shaven face had deepened a little, without sagging, and he did not take Sand's hand.

Sand withdrew the hand and placed it once more on the parcel containing the camera. The parcel completed his feeling of foolishness, like a superfluous picnic lunch. Jacobi observed it, black eyes unblinking.

"You know about the interview, then?" Sand shifted his gaze to a cot against the wall which, with a washstand, table, and Jacobi's chair, did nothing to offset the ascetic emptiness of the room. Jacobi did not answer. Behind him, through the open window, a green kite tilted crazily against the city sky and disappeared. Then a pigeon came, wheeling on swift, cracking wings before settling in anger on a low skylight above. "Marat said—"

Jacobi rose abruptly from the chair, clutching his biceps muscles with opposite hands. "What did you hope to gain by this?" he asked.

"An interview." Sand could not focus on his own position. "But I think I've gotten myself into some sort of trap," he muttered.

"Yes, you have. We know you're an enemy agent."

"Agent?"

"Yes. You were betrayed by the man who contacted Marat for you. This man also suggested how you might be put to use. That's why you're here."

"But I'm not an agent. Gleize must have lied to him!"

"It's much too late to plead innocence, Mr. Sand." Jacobi stopped short in his pacing of the room and peered closely at Sand's face. "No, you're no longer the innocent young man I remember." There was a sharp note of disappointment in his tone. He resumed his pacing.

"Please believe me," Sand said. "I'm not an agent. I did want an interview, for a wire service, but, more than that, I wanted to talk to you."

"Why?"

"I don't know."

Jacobi snorted.

"Well, it's hard to explain," Sand blurted. "I wanted to hear you once more on the subject of the Party." He offered a cigarette, which Jacobi did not bother to decline. "Marat told me certain things, but Marat—"

"Marat!" Jacobi interrupted. "Marat is a demagogue, and he exaggerates. You can't trust Marat. Even the Party doesn't trust him. But he is useful to us, a man like that, a voice like that, and people follow him like lemmings. Yet Marat is an individual, he can't be controlled, and one day he's going to find himself where I am now." He grimaced and punched one hand into the other, turning to Sand as if he had just noticed him. "No, you couldn't be an agent. No agent would try a stupid trick like this."

Sand tried to smile. "I give you my word for it," he said.

"Your word? I haven't taken anyone's word for anything in years." He shrugged. "What does it matter? You're too honest for your own good, Barney." They shook hands, and Jacobi, studying him, laughed. "Marat's put you through the mill, then, hasn't he?—that's his psychological approach. It wasn't enough to get you up here, he had to make a convert of you too!" Jacobi laughed again, a short hard sound that scarcely parted his lips. "So you're coming around to the Party view, then?"

"I don't think so. But I see more clearly why it exists, and its appeal for people."

"Do you? For me it becomes less clear each day."

"Yes, I suppose it does."

"No, Sand, I'm trying to feel sorry for myself." Jacobi leaned back against the window sill. "But the Party is a symptom of a basic situation—the people, even in the most primitive countries, are awakening to their rights. And in this century they are going to take those rights, whether or not the powers of East and West destroy each other." The words came angrily, didactically, and there had returned to Jacobi's face the sure, set quality that Sand remembered. "This world awakening is the great historical force of our time. The Party grew out of it, and even exploited it, but one day will find that it can no longer be controlled. Humanity, like Marat, is too perverse to be controlled." Excited, he was breathing heavily.

"I'm not sure I understand," Sand murmured. "I mean, why you fought so long for a cause you recognize as—well, selfish."

"It wasn't selfish, not in the beginning. It was international, but not truly political." He paused, reflective. "We wanted to believe that human beings would rise to the high principles of a cause, and they do, as long as the cause is not in power. But once in power, principles soon become political weapons, and they are abused. The Christian martyrs, had they lived in another century, might have led the Inquisition." He sat down heavily in the chair.

"But a moment ago you said, 'We know you're an enemy agent.' In other words, you still think of yourself—"

Jacobi frowned. "That's true," he said, "I did. But now you are dealing with the individual confusion of a defeated man." He hesitated. "Confusion is our natural state, I suppose, and we're dangerous without it. But it's a very new thing to me." He smiled tightly, unhappily.

Sand said nothing. He knew now that he had counted on Jacobi to clarify the disordered pattern of his concepts, unwilling to face the fact that no simple choice existed and that even at best, as Jacobi himself had come to realize, there would always be a mist of shifting grays to torment an honest man. Jacobi could not help him any more than he could help Jacobi, and would leave him to seek his solutions by himself.

And Jacobi, watching him, as if he had shared his thought, said, "But we haven't much time, Sand. Where is Marat?"

"He's giving me forty minutes with you," Sand said. "We must have nearly half an hour left."

"What happens then?"

"I'm not sure."

"You're not worried?"

"Yes, I am. Are you?"

"There isn't much left for me to worry about. I could have escaped if I'd wanted to. There's only one guard, and he wouldn't stop me."

"How do you know?"

"Marat told me. He came to see me some time ago."

"He *told* you that, Jacobi?"

"He knows I won't run. Where would I go, Sand, and for what? The flight would only be a proof of guilt." Jacobi got to his feet again and started pacing. "Marat and I were friends. He has a curious concept of friendship, but it's there. He said he would be disappointed to see an old soldier run. He said the Party owed me a little effort, a little ingenuity, at least, and that he would see to that himself. He was being cynical, of course, but he meant what he said."

"You mean you're just waiting here for him to do something?"

"Yes. What choice have I, really? And I may as well have the satisfaction of having done my duty by the Party, since it finds this necessary."

"Jacobi, you're confused. You can't mean that, you—"

"Don't forget what I said about confusion. It's the sign of the healthy mind." Jacobi winced. "No, you don't understand how the Party works, you'll never understand it. You're trying to do your own thinking, just as I did, Barney. The Party is not for you, do you hear?"

Sand nodded. "I've known it all along," he said half to himself. "I didn't trust my judgment." He gazed intently at Jacobi's tortured face. "I trust it now, though."

"And besides," Jacobi added, "you have a country to go to, and to serve, if you wish." Fretful, he slapped his pockets in search of cigarettes.

"I'm not convinced our country is in the right these days," Sand said, not quite believing this himself but astonished at Jacobi's reaction.

"Does that mean you can't serve it?" Jacobi shouted, rising. "You may as well say that you wouldn't help your child out of a pig trough because he was stupid enough to blunder into it! If I was in your position, with all your advantages, I wouldn't be wandering around Europe the way you are! I'd be home in America doing something about whatever I thought was wrong! It's people like you who cede the country to the ones who will do it harm, people like you who—"

"You don't have to abuse me," Sand interrupted quietly. He wanted to be angry but could not. Observing the raging, frustrated man before him, he felt only regret. How different it had been at their first meeting, the assistance they had given each other, which now, in greater need, they could not duplicate.

"All right," Jacobi said. But clearly he was not sorry about his violence. There was something else. Jacobi had sunk into his chair and now sat absolutely quiet. After a time he remarked in a different voice, "I wish I could have died in action without ever having had this chance to think. I regarded myself as a martyr of some sort, since I was willing to give everything to a cause I considered just, even my right to live and die in my own country. I never considered my personal reasons at all, it never occurred to me that self-sacrifice and self-justification could be synonymous." He glanced at Sand, licking his lips. "I remember how, talking to you that afternoon long ago, I kept thinking how much of life I'd never had—a wife, a home, my own children, all the things you people take for granted—and that I'd never really been a child at all. I mean, the childhood you knew, the swimming and fishing, the boats on the blue waters of so many summers. I kept thinking about those boats, far out from shore on a bright clean sea of blue and white. You gave me a sort of daydream of another life, Barney, and it blurred everything I did." Embarrassed, he lit the cigarette bent by his heavy fingers. One of his shoelaces had come untied, and a thin white ankle shone above one fallen sock. Behind him the pigeons came and went, complaining.

"Did you know that your father came to see me when I

left America, and said that he still considered himself in my debt, and offered help? Do you think he could have been sincere?"

"Yes, I do. But then, the gentleman's code might be simply the self-justification you referred to."

"Only when it adjusts one's ethics to one's interests."

"I know what you mean—"

"Oh, cynicism can be very beneficial," Jacobi said quietly. "It weeds out the unhealthy idealists, most of them." He glanced at Sand. "Because if one clings too desperately to one ideal, one will sooner or later sacrifice a second, then a third and fourth, and do more harm than good. Idealism loses its spontaneity and hardens. Then it is fanatic, and it is wrong."

"Are you in doubt about yourself?"

"I don't know. Perhaps I'm trying to demonstrate to myself, and no doubt to you, that my course in life was the product of reflection, that I—" He leaped to his feet again; a cry of pain twisted from his throat. "No, I've been right, I've done right!"

He was facing the window, addressing the world, and his voice assumed the vibrating timbre it had held before. "The people are awakening all over the earth, like hordes of locusts, and the men who stand in their path will be crushed, do you hear, consumed!" Jacobi orated wildly, desperately, but suddenly he stopped, and his arms fell back to his sides. The spark was gone. From beyond the window there fell on his silence the distant noises of the world, a world that went on and on and on, transforming itself in its slow fashion without him.

Then he moved toward Sand quickly, purposefully, his expression calm again, and cold. "Come on," he said, "I'm going to get you out of here."

"Marat thinks I'm cooperating," Sand said. "He won't do anything to me."

"You *are* cooperating, Sand. Is that what you want?" He

snapped Sand's parcel from his hand. "What's this?" he demanded.

"A camera. For the interview." Sand adjusted his collar.

"A camera. He's thought of everything, hasn't he? I suppose you paid for it too."

"Yes. Or rather, he paid for it. He has my money," Sand admitted, sheepish.

Jacobi shook his head. "Sand," he said, "do you have any idea how much trouble you're in? Do you think they're going to let you walk away from here knowing where I am, much less any information I might have given you? Marat knows I wouldn't tell you anything, but the others—suppose the others want to take no chances? Do you know that no matter how much you cooperate you'll still have knowledge that they want suppressed?"

"I don't intend to cooperate," Sand said, "so it doesn't matter."

"Just answer me this," Jacobi pursued, as if he hadn't heard. "Is there any person in this city who knows where you are? Is there anybody who would know where to bring help even if he knew you needed it? In other words, is there anybody who would know immediately if you were to disappear?"

"No," Sand said. Except Rudi Gleize, he thought, if Olivier was right, and he's followed us here; but Rudi has betrayed me already, and wouldn't help me now.

"I didn't think so. You don't even know what their plan is, do you?"

"No," Sand said, "I don't."

Above, the pigeon's feet scratched irritably on the skylight.

"They think you're an agent. They are going to 'find' us here together so that the Party members can be told that the former leader Jacobi is in league with American espionage and working with the government. And they are going to do it at a time when the Party is in trouble and the rank and file excited about informers because of that government raid." He pointed at a newspaper on the table, then jerked his thumb toward the door. "And the guard. I know him. He's a hand-picked 'witness,' a Resistance hero during the war, a respected district leader, an honest worker. And the camera, to record the evidence." Jacobi laughed his brief laugh of rage. "It must have amused Marat to have you pay for it."

"How do you know all this?"

"I've worked with the Party for a long time, Sand."

"Suppose I prove to them I'm not an agent."

"I doubt if you could. And even if you did, at this late date, they would carry out the plan. Who in the Party would believe your denial, even if you were around to express it?"

"Well, why do they go to all this trouble, then? Why not simply announce your guilt?"

"Not in this country. Not yet. They aren't sure enough of their strength to crucify me by accusation alone. They want a good case, with witnesses, photographs, the whole business."

"And all to prove a lie," Sand muttered.

"Yes. Why not? We've never balked at means to an end, if the end is desirable." Again Jacobi pronounced the "we" with a hard pride.

"You find the end desirable?"

"It's of no importance what I think." Jacobi gazed at him. "If you hadn't come, Sand, I would have gone along with them without a murmur. Sitting here so many weeks alone, I became resigned. Perhaps that was their intention. But now— No, I won't accept disgrace. Instead I will do the job for them, and hope they will deal fairly with me after I am dead, for I have the choice of disgrace or death." His voice was mono-tone, undramatic. "And please don't ask me again if I believe in the Party. I don't want to think any more. I only know that my life has gone to the Party, and that disgrace would remove the meaning my life has had. I am speaking hypocrisy, and I know it, and it hurts; but when you reach my age you will understand that the agony of a wasted life is the most unbearable of all." Abruptly he turned his back on Sand and bent to tie his shoelace.

"Now," he snapped, "let's get moving. How many are there out there?"

"Marat and the guard. Jacobi, wait a minute—"

"There'll be others before long," Jacobi said. "We've got to hurry." He put the chair beneath the skylight window and, climbing up, propped it open.

"I'm sure there's no escape that way." Sand wavered, trapped between his peril and the import of Jacobi's plan.

"No. But escape won't be necessary. Bring the camera."

Sand followed Jacobi through the skylight hatch to the roof. When he got to his feet, Jacobi was already standing on the parapet with his back to the street. "You have your story," he said calmly to Sand, "and you'll have a picture to go with it. Is the camera ready?"

"Yes," Sand said. "I won't let you do this."

"I don't see how you can stop me. If you come any closer, I am going to jump, so you may as well cooperate, and save yourself." Jacobi spoke with tight satisfaction, his black eyes burning. "I am going to shout and draw a crowd, and the police, and they will protect you from harm. And in return, I want you to publish your story and a picture to prove it, and say that Jacobi, suffering from nervous depression, died by his own hand, loyal to the Party, and that his last words expressed his devotion to the people's cause." He licked his lips. "The story may not be necessary, since the Party will probably not go to the unnecessary trouble of defaming me. But I'm afraid I do not trust it. I want to make sure."

"I'm not going to write the story. They'll use any story against you." Sand felt sick to his stomach, and could not look the other man in the eyes. Instead he turned his gaze down

into the street, as if by staring intently at the concrete details
of the scene this overwhelming act might be made to take
place beyond his sight. He hoped that, turning once again to
the cold eyes, he might find them irresolute, afraid.

"Raise it," Jacobi said. "The story is true."

The street Sand saw was typical of certain outer areas of
the city. It was gray and foreshortened and dog-stained, with
brown water running in the gutters between its ill-matched
buildings. Below their roof, in an adjoining junkyard, a band
of cats had congregated, and one stretched with deceptive lan-
guor as its fellow, stalking past in irritable solitude, moved out
of view behind it. On the corner two men idled, a postman
and a cripple with a spavined dog, and, talking, they gazed
past Sand to the point where Jacobi stood.

Then Marat came around the corner with two other men.
"Raise it," the voice repeated.

And Sand turned toward Jacobi again, aligning the other's
shoulders with the city beyond. Across the tumbled rooftops
he could see the spires of Sainte-Clothilde, but they were far
away, too far away to be meaningful or real or even to place
his whereabouts in his mind. Beneath a broken autumn sky
the city sloped away from him, its roofs crouching down behind one another toward the river, and there came to his ears
its endless murmur, guttural and patient, soulless. The lost
wail of a fire wagon, *pang-pawng, pang-pawng-g-g,* died swiftly
in the distance and, nearer, a child called and a cat complained
and a woman in black, sprawled on her elbows in the window
opposite, answered a remark from the dark room behind her
with a strident, derisive, profoundly humorless laugh. She too
watched Jacobi, noncommittal, without hope, as if she had
long since abandoned the idea that man might do anything of
interest in her presence.

Now Sand looked full into Jacobi's face. It had gone white,

a dirty powder white like the face of a clown, but the black eyes did not waver. And this terrible self-control banished in Sand the last of the apathy induced by Marat, the fatalism. Fear for Jacobi's life, for himself, for the life they shared, seared through him, gutted him, and he sank down onto the parapet, clutching the raw red brick of it with his hand. At the same time his mind ran blindly on, screaming back at him, This isn't real, this isn't you here on this roof, this isn't meaningful at all, and his voice creaked, "It won't work," to the wind, "there must be some better way than this."

"Please raise the camera," the thin lips said, "for your own sake, if not mine." Jacobi was balanced on the roof edge. Below, a child questioned its mother, and down the street there came a shout.

Sand stared at the camera in his lap and located the hard white face in the lens. Then the mouth in the face became a hole, and he heard a hoarse, furious roar, wordless, agonized— all the helpless rage of humankind. And below in the bleak barrens of the street the people ran to hear Jacobi, numbers of them, eager, anxious, as if they had lain in wait behind the walls until he had chosen to summon them. The woman across the way was screeching for God and witnesses, and there rose the sound of pounding feet on the raw pavement, and a cacophony of doors and shutters interspersed with a babel of shouts, the bark of a dog, and, from somewhere, the cry of children.

But in a moment all individual din had died away, submerged in the general tumult, as if Jacobi's cry had swollen, voices upon voices, until the noise of humanity rose in protest over the roofs and flooded past him, remorseless and insane. Here were Jacobi's human hordes, and Sand imagined them, unleashed by his cry, swarming through the city and spreading out across the world. Already the building shook with the

weight of their feet upon the stairs, and then the skylight shat-
tered and he saw the shaggy head of Marat erupt, wild and
demonic, through the hole.

Marat was howling out his contempt, his great face twisted
with rage. "So that's it, eh, Jacobi! So that's the way the old
soldier is going to go, eh! Well, go and be damned, then!"

Jacobi stiffened, then stepped down onto the roof. He
seemed bewildered. Below him the din diminished to an angry
moan, like wind around a building, and, beyond, the green kite
danced, high in the harsh November air of some far, oblivious
street.

Marat had now emerged from the skylight and stood gazing at them, breathing in hoarse gasps. "Let me have the camera," he said to Sand.

Sand dropped the camera into the street, and the crowd
surged back from it, shouting.

"No," Jacobi muttered, moving forward. "They're not
going to get away with this." He brushed past Sand, unnatu-
rally intent. Marat waited for him. His right hand started toward his pocket as Jacobi, too quick, covered the final yards in
one lithe spurt. He knocked Marat flat. Marat sat up on his
elbows, the revolver pointed at Jacobi.

"Go on," Jacobi said. "Put an end to it."

Marat spun the revolver on his trigger finger as Jacobi
turned and kicked the hinged window from the skylight and,
placing his hands on the frame, dropped through. Then Marat
replaced the revolver in his pocket and, rolling over, peered
down through the skylight, his cut, bloody mouth hanging
open in a sort of smile. There was a tumult on the stairs.
Marat waited a moment before shouting out, "Look out, boys,
here he comes!" Then he got to his feet and went to the edge
of the roof, still smiling.

Jacobi pitched out into the street and fell to his knees at
the feet of the crowd. Behind him, shoving at the onlookers,

came Marat's men, their voices rising above the clamor and
the angry horns of automobiles attempting to enter the street.
"Grab him!" one yelled; and the other bellowed, "He's dangerous, he's a lunatic!" This man had a bleeding nose.

The people jockeyed for positions, pressing toward Jacobi,
groaning forth their excitement and suspicion. "Lunatic!" one
cried, and, "Murderer!" screeched another, more imaginative,
and an old woman called repeatedly, "Police!" And Jacobi, on
his feet again, rumpled and reeling, stared at the people, un-
believing, and then he too was shouting, incomprehensible in
dazed English, until a voice cried out, "American! Go home!"

Marat's men closed in on him. Jacobi chopped wildly at
the people nearest him and cleared a path. Backing toward
the free end of the street, he called out to them to listen, but
still they came for him, the ranks behind leaning forward on
the leaders. Then he turned and ran, and the people pursued
him as far as the corner. Behind Marat's men Rudi Gleize,
funereal in black, scurried along the wall.

Sand turned his back to the street, breathing deep to clear
away an inner mist of tears. Marat, mute, stared after Jacobi,
but in a moment vented his emotion in a grating sigh. "That
hurts," he muttered. "That hurts."

"You let him go," Sand pondered dully.

"He escaped." Marat did not turn around. "He deserved a
chance, a man like that. But he's beaten now, and we'll find
him again, no matter how far he goes or where he hides."

The crowd was drifting apart, and the building was quiet.
Sand glanced at Marat, who was watching two policemen
moving away down the street, stood gaunt and still against a
gray yellow distance. The sun rolled weakly through the clouds
and again was gone. Then he knew what Marat was waiting
for. He slipped swiftly toward the skylight, and, when Marat
shouted, ran for it and jumped down through, hurting his leg
on Jacobi's fallen chair.

He won't dare shoot, he thought, he won't dare—but he scrambled in panic to his feet and fled through the door and down the stairs, hearing the crash of Marat's leap behind him. Sand skirted the wall and, reaching the bottom, ran out and across the street to the opposite sidewalk. The policemen paused to stare at him as Marat appeared in the doorway. Sand started toward them.

"Sand!" Marat called.

"Keep your distance," Sand said to him as he came up. He nodded toward the policemen, who watched them, undecided.

Marat paused, standing in the gutter. "You forgot your billfold," he said, and tossed it.

"How careless of me," Sand said, his mouth still dry.

"About your story, Sand—I'd be careful about what I say if I were you."

"Are you threatening me, Marat?"

"Yes," Marat said, "I am."

"You're not in a very strong position any more," Sand told him, his terror displaced by a cumulative anger. "You're in trouble, Marat. Suppose I write my story, and tell how you outsmarted yourself from the beginning, and let Jacobi escape on purpose?"

"The Party wouldn't believe it."

"It wouldn't have to believe it to use the story against you, would it?"

Marat kicked irritably at the curb. "Or against Jacobi," he said. "We'll use you and your story against Jacobi."

"That's not my concern."

"I happen to think it is. You risked your neck for him when you dropped that camera."

"You plan to use me anyhow, isn't that true? You have witnesses to the meeting. You might even say that I helped Jacobi escape."

Marat grinned despite himself. "You've gotten a lot smarter, my friend," he said.

"I have you to thank for that," Sand said. "You taught me the hard way." He glanced at the policemen, who had turned away again. "Look, Marat, I don't intend to wait here with you until the police have gone, so let's not waste time. I can't help Jacobi, but neither do I want to be used to hurt him, so I won't write my story—not until I read in the papers that some of this business has been held against him. Is that clear enough?"

"Mm-hm." Marat eyed a cold blade of sunlight that overtook them in the street. The breeze swirled with it, fell away again, and Marat shoved his hands into his pockets. Standing in the gutter, he seemed forlorn.

"Which way are you going?" Sand asked.

Marat stepped onto the sidewalk and walked backward slowly in the direction taken by Jacobi. "Come along," he said. "We can discuss this as we go."

"I'm going the other way."

Marat stopped.

"You'd better keep going, Marat. You still have Rudi Gleize to deal with."

Marat nodded his head, a rueful expression creasing his bony face. "I see. He was here, then, our fat Rudi?"

"Yes. He went after Jacobi."

"Thanks," Marat said. He held out his hand, and Sand took it. "I think we understand each other, my friend. But I warn you to stay out of this from now on, in print or otherwise."

"Give my regards to Rudi," Sand said.

"I mean to." Marat started away, then broke into the long swift run of a hunting animal and disappeared.

16

Sand went away in the opposite direction, moving rapidly himself and pausing at corners to see if he was being followed. Directed to the nearest Métro station—GAÎTÉ, it read—he determined from its chart just where he was, though he still did not know where he was going. He wandered on foot to the Boulevard Montparnasse and made his way down the hill to the Luxembourg Gardens. There he sank onto a bench, where he sat for a long time in a trance.

Its over, his mind repeated to him dully; it's all over and you're free.

Around him red-jacketed children hunted out the last horse chestnuts in the fallen leaves, and one little boy, biting into one, scowled horribly at Sand. Sand laughed aloud, and was startled by the sound. From down the path a woman called the boy, and he skipped away backward, waving. "Au revoir," he called, "au revoir!" his voice as faint as a wisp of autumn smoke among the bright cries and colors beneath the trees.

Beyond, as the sun failed in the west, the gold leaf of late afternoon climbed from the sidewalks of the rue Vaugirard to the crests of its weathered façades. An old man beside Sand on the bench was consuming his tempered life with deep, slow, avid breaths, kneading a bag of bread crumbs for a grum-

bling gray pigeon, and when the bag was empty Sand stood
again and asked him for the hour.

*Mais qu'est-ce que ça peut te faire, mon petit, puisque ça
change tout le temps?* said the voice of long ago. But the old
man had not said that. He only started backward in alarm and
whispered, "Excuse me, young man, I have no idea, though
surely it must be late."

What use to you to know the time, poor man, since it
changes every moment?

Sand thanked the man and left the gardens, continuing
downhill to Odéon. Though tired, he dreaded the prospect of
his dark apartment and could not make himself go home. He
suffered a sense of unreality, and needed to talk, feel close to
people. And since, besides, he wanted to inquire about Olivier,
and offer help, he went to the rue des Grands Augustins.

On the landing he hesitated, feeling his beard with fingers
dry with dirt, then straightened his appearance as best he could
and knocked. Lise opened the door, then half closed it again
and stared at him.

"Hello, Lise," he said to her. "I'd like to see Olivier."

"No," she said, searching his face. "No, you have caused
enough trouble as it is, we want nothing more to do with you!
Olivier has done nothing, he is a child, he is not like Marat or
Jacobi!" She came forward a little and touched his face with
her fingertips, peering into his eyes. "No, and he is not like
you, my poor Sand, for you're not the way you were." She
backed quickly into the apartment. "My Olivier was beaten,
he is very sick! Now go away!"

"I'd like to help," Sand said. The door was closing. "Good-
by, Lise." He started down the stairs, clutching the banister
in the dim light, but her voice caught up with him on the
landing below.

"Bar-ney? You understand me, don't you, about Olivier?
He must be kept from harm, a soul like that, he has no place

in their world, your world! You can only help him if you stay
away! Bar-ney? I—I'll come and see you soon, we can be together, you can tell me about Jacobi, and we—Tell me where
you live, and I will come." She had crept out onto the landing,
peering down into the darkness for some sign of him. For a
moment he paused, then pretended he hadn't heard her and
kept going.

Before, he thought, when I was the untempered idealist, I
might have accepted her and betrayed Olivier again. He nodded at the concierge, shawled and vigilant at her window, and
passed out into the street.

He went down to the river. The days were shorter now,
and in the air, expectant, there hung a hint of night. Alone
on the corner he watched the heedless passers-by and the
booksellers pacing back and forth before their stalls. One buttoned his jacket up and moved to close down for the day, and
Sand went on. Walking still, he made his way west along the
Seine to the Pont du Carrousel.

In his own street the dark had come, and his concierge
peered at him suspiciously before she recognized him. Her
"Bonsoir, m'sieu" was interrogative, but he only nodded. She
gave him letters and watched him climb the stairs.

His apartment was still and cold. He did not have the energy to go out again for food, and instead removed his shoes
and jacket and got into the bed to warm himself. His mail, he
thought, would tide him over into sleep. Flat on his back, he
opened a letter from his father.

Dear Edwin,

I was delighted to learn, from your letter of some weeks
ago, that you have not ruled out a career in the foreign
service. You know, of course, how very much it would
please me to have you carry on when I retire, and all the
more so in the light of a recent development.

It appears that I have a black mark on my record, and for a reason I find most disheartening after twenty-odd years of service. In brief, I was reported by an unidentified witness to have engaged in a "secret" conversation aboard his ship with the deported Party leader, Jacobi, in 1948, and to have "kept it hidden" ever since. In connection with advancement to a higher post, I was asked to explain this meeting satisfactorily. I told the truth, that for *personal* reasons—and I described these—I felt obliged to offer my *personal* assistance to Jacobi. Perhaps this was naïve on my part, but, if so, it is a naïveté I cannot feel ashamed of, whatever comes of it. In any case, the truth was construed by a body of small men as an act "not consistent with the best interests of America." I was not approved for the ambassadorship in question, and was placed on the inactive list, pending further investigation.

Of course I intend to fight, less out of pride, I hope, than out of duty to my family and, as I see it, to the nation—a nation in danger of falling, at a time of terrible danger, into the hands of these small men, these modern "politicians," with their cheap bag of tricks and their cheap chauvinism. They are not true public servants, but only so many shrill, irresponsible heads on the hydra of public opinion.

I recall a phrase you once attributed to Jacobi—the Great Twentieth-Century War. It is very apt, I think, no matter where one stands. We are at war on every front, of mind and heart and soul, and we must believe, to know what we must fight, and perhaps we must suffer, as I have, a little late, to understand that what we believe can never be infallible. I trouble you with all this, Barney, not only because I am upset, but in the hope that one day you will help to vindicate my faith in the true greatness of our country.

Sand dropped the letter to the floor. He lay there in a stupor of directionless, dull rage, directionless because he could not focus on the issues. There was only his father's face, the cool, humorous, dedicated eyes; and these eyes merged with those of Jacobi, of Olivier, of Marat standing in the gutter, of every man at bay before himself.

Against the ceiling of his room, he sorted out impressions of his journey, the stark avenues and alleys, the fat soiled women and thin soiled men, thin cats, thin children, the sooted trees and empty faces. Somewhere his countryman Jacobi lay in hiding, and Marat hunted in the people's name, and Gleize slipped down his predatory path. And Sand, he thought—what is to become of the idealistic Sand?

Have I been so intent on life because I am afraid—and am I afraid because life can be destroyed, or because, if it can be destroyed, it must be meaningless? The dark gave back nothing by way of resolution, and after a time he fell asleep.

He was awakened fifteen hours later by the telephone at his bed, the brassy clamor of the surface world.

"Barney?" his editor said. "Is that you, Barney?"

"How did you know I was back?" Barney said.

"I've been calling you every morning for two weeks. I was just about to notify the Embassy. Are you all right? Look, did you see him?"

"Yes."

"You're promoted. Now get on over here while I still believe you. I'll get a stenographer ready, and some coffee. How soon can you get here? Hello? You still there?"

"I'm not coming," Barney said, and lay back on his pillow.

"What are you talking about? Listen, you're promoted, you'll get a raise, a bonus, maybe a journalist's award, for Christ's sake!"

Barney was silent.

"Name your price, then," the editor said. "I'm coming over right away."

"Never mind. I haven't got a story."

"You saw him, didn't you? Don't do this to me, goddam it—"

"I'm sorry, but I haven't got a story. That's final."

"By God, I'll fire you, Sand!"

"All right," Barney said, and put down the receiver.

He got slowly out of bed and went to the window and gazed out upon the autumn day, clear and windless in the sun, and strangely quiet. And even when, remembering how he had wandered here, he picked at his filthy clothes and stroked his chin, he could not believe that the weeks gone by were over.

He told himself that his thoughts had not yet fallen into place, and undressed, shaved, and took a shower. The shower troubled him because it relaxed him more than he felt he deserved, because he emerged from it singing "Mademoiselle de Paris." Where had he heard that song so recently—was it Olivier? He smiled, and observed the smile with detachment in the mirror.

What's come over you? he wondered. You weren't so goddam full of fun last night. Are you so relieved that the search is over, that you're safe, is that it? He reminded himself of Jacobi and his father, and scowled at his reflection. At the same time he was unable to retrieve the sense of doom of the night before, he was pleased to be alive and free again, he was even confident.

Perplexed, he dressed in fine fresh clothes and went down stairs and up the street to the café. There he sat on the terrace in the sun and, smoking a cigarette over coffee and croissants, reread his father's letter.

"I trouble you with all this, Barney, not only because I am

upset ..." Sand struck the letter down across the table edge. Barney, he thought—that's the first time he's ever admitted that I'm called Barney, and for him it's a first admission of defeat.

How alike they were, his father and Jacobi, in so very many ways—and now they shared the wormwood of ingratitude from their corrupted causes, and the exile of all uncompromising men. He was angry for them, and saddened by their personal defeat, which he could do nothing to retrieve. Their causes, by comparison, seemed remote and unimportant, like accounts of distant happenings in small, cold print. Reality was this cigarette, this cup of coffee, at a table on a terrace in the sun. He wondered if he himself might not be running from all causes, frightened off by the past month's danger and confusion, or if his mind might not have hardened, or whether in some mysterious fashion his return to the starting point had obviated his entire search. His clearest impression of the day before was the scene in the Luxembourg Gardens, the red and green and gold, the chestnuts which, since the Indian summers of his childhood, had stood for the turn of autumn, the quiet-burning days when the world did not matter but the earth, and one felt restless and alone with time.

And because this was so he felt selfish and ashamed, and when he looked up in time to see his editor approach the doorway of his building he taunted himself, Why don't you sell it to him, then, your miserable story, get your wretched bonus, your award—why not? He rapped coins for his coffee down upon the table, and the waiter hurried toward him. But when the editor reappeared, and turned in the other direction, Sand kept his fingers on the coins and watched him go.

The waiter, scraping coins into his palm, inquired if monsieur desired something else. Barney shook his head. He watched an enormous blue balloon, which came abreast of him on small boy's legs, with small arms wrapped around it.

Then a pair of round brown eyes gazed at him, over the nose pressed into the balloon. The child was an Arab urchin, so ingrained with grime that his collar seemed a growth on his gray skin. He wore outside his jacket a baroque Moroccan belt of the sort hawked everywhere by Arab vendors, but his was of a thin, cheap make, wan red with rough white stitching, and, bunching his shapeless jacket, served only to bind to him his air of poverty.

He's proud of that belt, Barney thought, though it's probably stolen from his father. But the point is, he's trying— Trying for what? In the face of the future he would know, where did he find the nerve to try, much less the strength? It didn't matter. The red belt, like the blue balloon, disturbed him not because it seemed so out of place, so garish against the rags, but because the boy's faith in it somehow reflected upon himself.

He got up from the table. Perhaps his father was beyond his help, as Jacobi had been yesterday, and Olivier. Yet he had to try again, tomorrow in America; he had to keep on trying. And perhaps that trying would come to something in the end, though he might never see the sense in it.

The balloon bounced silently before him, and he punted it toward its small, onrushing owner.

"Ça, alors!" an old gentleman exclaimed, and lashed out with his cane at the huge balloon. The old man had missed on purpose, but a streetcleaner touched a cigarette to it— bang!—and winked at Barney. "Va-t'en, négrillon," he jeered at the Arab child. This man was heavy-faced with drink, in dirty work clothes, idling.

The child backed off, teeth bared, but the old gentleman danced forward, brandishing his cane. "Salaud!" he screeched. "Brute, idiot, animal!"

The streetcleaner's eyes widened in dull, red surprise, and searched Barney's own for understanding. They exchanged a look scraped bare of all pretense. Yes, I know you, Barney thought, I'm not angry with you. The man, surrounded by the crowd, gazed after Barney as he crossed the street.

He went downhill and through the Jardin de Paris, along the Champs Elysées. The trees seemed taller now, and thin, and wind-whirled yellow linden leaves, like spiny hearts, caught at his shirt, spun, fell away. Near the Concorde he waved at passing taxis, but this was the headlong morning hour, and the taxis took no notice of him. They were caught in the heedless sweep of cars, big blind black cars of couriers of world affairs.

Peter Matthiessen was born in New York City in 1927 and had already begun his writing career by the time he graduated from Yale University in 1950. The following year, he was a founder of *The Paris Review*. Besides *At Play in the Fields of the Lord*, which was nominated for the National Book Award, he has published four other novels, including *Far Tortuga*. Mr. Matthiessen's unique career as a naturalist and explorer has resulted in numerous and widely acclaimed books of nonfiction, among them *The Tree Where Man Was Born* (with Eliot Porter), which was nominated for the National Book Award, and *The Snow Leopard*, which won it. His other works of nonfiction include *The Cloud Forest* and *Under the Mountain Wall* (which together received an Award of Merit from the National Institute of Arts and Letters), *The Wind Birds, Blue Meridian, Sand Rivers, In the Spirit of Crazy Horse, Indian Country*, and, most recently, *Men's Lives*. His novel-in-progress and a collection of his short stories will be published by Random House.